Edgar Rice Burroughs was gifted with a limitless imagination. With it he created an entire culture for a vast planet—many races, many peoples, strange creatures, and stranger plants, an entire history stretching back through eons of time and extending itself into the future with scientific inventions only dreamed of even in our own time.

His imagination was coupled with an ability to write startlingly graphic prose, vivid with color and excitement, seething with action, and rich with the barbaric splendor of bygone ages.

THUVIA, MAID OF MARS is the fourth book in a classic series of eleven volumes.

Edgar Rice Burroughs
MARS NOVELS

Published by Ballantine Books

A PRINCESS OF MARS
THE GODS OF MARS
THE WARLORD OF MARS
THUVIA, MAID OF MARS
THE CHESSMEN OF MARS
THE MASTER MIND OF MARS
A FIGHTING MAN OF MARS
SWORDS OF MARS
SYNTHETIC MEN OF MARS
LLANA OF GATHOL
JOHN CARTER OF MARS

THUVIA,
MAID OF MARS

Edgar Rice Burroughs

BALLANTINE BOOKS • NEW YORK

CONTENTS

THUVIA, MAID OF MARS

CHAPTER I

CARTHORIS AND THUVIA

UPON A MASSIVE bench of polished ersite beneath the gorgeous blooms of a giant pimalia a woman sat. Her shapely, sandalled foot tapped impatiently upon the jewel-strewn walk that wound beneath the stately sorapus trees across the scarlet sward of the royal gardens of Thuvan Dihn, Jeddak of Ptarth, as a dark-haired, red-skinned warrior bent low toward her, whispering heated words close to her ear.

"Ah, Thuvia of Ptarth," he cried, "you are cold even before the fiery blasts of my consuming love! No harder than your heart, nor colder is the hard, cold ersite of this thrice happy bench which supports your divine and fadeless form! Tell me, O Thuvia of Ptarth, that I may still hope—that though you do not love me now, yet some day, some day, my princess, I——"

The girl sprang to her feet with an exclamation of surprise and displeasure. Her queenly head was poised haughtily upon her smooth red shoulders. Her dark eyes looked angrily into those of the man.

"You forget yourself, and the customs of Barsoom, Astok," she said. "I have given you no right thus to address the daughter of Thuvan Dihn, nor have you won such a right."

The man reached suddenly forth and grasped her by the arm.

7

"You shall be my princess!" he cried. "By the breast of Issus, thou shalt, nor shall any other come between Astok, Prince of Dusar, and his heart's desire. Tell me that there is another, and I shall cut out his foul heart and fling it to the wild calots of the dead sea-bottoms!"

At touch of the man's hand upon her flesh the girl went pallid beneath her coppery skin, for the persons of the royal women of the courts of Mars are held but little less than sacred. The act of Astok, Prince of Dusar, was profanation. There was no terror in the eyes of Thuvia of Ptarth—only horror for the thing the man had done and for its possible consequences.

"Release me." Her voice was level—frigid.

The man muttered incoherently and drew her roughly toward him.

"Release me!" she repeated sharply, "or I call the guard, and the Prince of Dusar knows what that will mean."

Quickly he threw his right arm about her shoulders and strove to draw her face to his lips. With a little cry she struck him full in the mouth with the massive bracelets that circled her free arm.

"Calot!" she exclaimed, and then: "The guard! The guard! Hasten in protection of the Princess of Ptarth!"

In answer to her call a dozen guardsmen came racing across the scarlet sward, their gleaming long-swords naked in the sun, the metal of their accoutrements clanking against that of their leathern harness, and in their throats hoarse shouts of rage at the sight which met their eyes.

But before they had passed half across the royal garden to where Astok of Dusar still held the struggling girl in his grasp, another figure sprang from a cluster of dense foliage that half hid a golden fountain close at hand. A tall, straight youth he was, with black hair and keen grey eyes; broad of shoulder and narrow of hip; a clean-limbed fighting man. His skin was but faintly tinged with the copper colour that marks the red men of Mars from the other races of the dying planet—he was like them, and yet there was a subtle difference greater even than that which lay in his lighter skin and his grey eyes.

There was a difference, too, in his movements. He came on in great leaps that carried him so swiftly over the ground that the speed of the guardsmen was as nothing by comparison.

Astok still clutched Thuvia's wrist as the young warrior confronted him. The new-comer wasted no time and he spoke but a single word.

"Calot!" he snapped, and then his clenched fist landed beneath the other's chin, lifting him high into the air and depositing him in a crumpled heap within the centre of the pimalia bush beside the ersite bench.

Her champion turned toward the girl. "Kaor, Thuvia of Ptarth!" he cried. "It seems that fate timed my visit well."

"Kaor, Carthoris of Helium!" the princess returned the young man's greeting, "and what less could one expect of the son of such a sire?"

He bowed his acknowledgment of the compliment to his father, John Carter, Warlord of Mars. And then the guardsmen, panting from their charge, came up just as the Prince of Dusar, bleeding at the mouth, and with drawn sword, crawled from the entanglement of the pimalia.

Astok would have leaped to mortal combat with the son of Dejah Thoris, but the guardsmen pressed about him, preventing, though it was clearly evident that naught would have better pleased Carthoris of Helium.

"But say the word, Thuvia of Ptarth," he begged, "and naught will give me greater pleasure than meting to this fellow the punishment he has earned."

"It cannot be, Carthoris," she replied. "Even though he has forfeited all claim upon my consideration, yet is he the guest of the jeddak, my father, and to him alone may he account for the unpardonable act he has committed."

"As you say, Thuvia," replied the Heliumite. "But

afterward he shall account to Carthoris, Prince of Helium, for this affront to the daughter of my father's friend." As he spoke, though, there burned in his eyes a fire that proclaimed a nearer, dearer cause for his championship of this glorious daughter of Barsoom.

The maid's cheek darkened beneath the satin of her transparent skin, and the eyes of Astok, Prince of Dusar, darkened, too, as he read that which passed unspoken between the two in the royal gardens of the jeddak.

"And thou to me," he snapped at Carthoris, answering the young man's challenge.

The guard still surrounded Astok. It was a difficult position for the young officer who commanded it. His prisoner was the son of a mighty jeddak; he was the guest of Thuvan Dihn—until but now an honoured guest upon whom every royal dignity had been showered. To arrest him forcibly could mean naught else than war, and yet he had done that which in the eyes of the Ptarth warrior merited death.

The young man hesitated. He looked toward his princess. She, too, guessed all that hung upon the action of the coming moment. For many years Dusar and Ptarth had been at peace with each other. Their great merchant ships plied back and forth between the larger cities of the two nations. Even now, far above the gold-shot scarlet dome of the jeddak's palace, she could see the huge bulk of a giant freighter taking its majestic way through the thin Barsoomian air toward the west and Dusar.

By a word she might plunge these two mighty nations into a bloody conflict that would drain them of their bravest blood and their incalculable riches, leaving them all helpless against the inroads of their envious and less powerful neighbours, and at last a prey to the savage green hordes of the dead sea-bottoms.

No sense of fear influenced her decision, for fear is seldom known to the children of Mars. It was rather a sense of the responsibility that she, the daughter of their jeddak, felt for the welfare of her father's people.

"I called you, Padwar," she said to the lieutenant of the guard, "to protect the person of your princess, and to keep the peace that must not be violated within the royal gardens of the jeddak. That is all. You will escort me to the palace, and the Prince of Helium will accompany me."

Without another glance in the direction of Astok she turned, and taking Carthoris' proffered hand, moved slowly toward the massive marble pile that housed the ruler of Ptarth and his glittering court. On either side marched a file of guardsmen. Thus Thuvia of Ptarth found a way out of a dilemma, escaping the necessity of placing her father's royal guest under forcible restraint, and at the same time separating the two princes, who otherwise would have been at each other's throat the moment she and the guard had departed.

Beside the pimalia stood Astok, his dark eyes narrowed to mere slits of hate beneath his lowering brows as he watched the retreating forms of the woman who had aroused the fiercest passions of his nature and the man whom he now believed to be the one who stood between his love and its consummation.

As they disappeared within the structure Astok shrugged his shoulders, and with a murmured oath crossed the gardens toward another wing of the building where he and his retinue were housed.

That night he took formal leave of Thuvan Dihn, and though no mention was made of the happening within the garden, it was plain to see through the cold mask of the jeddak's courtesy that only the customs of royal hospitality restrained him from voicing the contempt he felt for the Prince of Dusar.

Carthoris was not present at the leave-taking, nor was Thuvia. The ceremony was as stiff and formal as court etiquette could make it, and when the last of the Dusarians clambered over the rail of the battleship that had brought them upon this fateful visit to the court of Ptarth, and the mighty engine of destruction had risen slowly from the ways of the landing-stage, a note of relief was apparent in the voice of Thuvan Dihn as he turned to one of his officers with a word of comment upon a subject foreign to that which had been uppermost in the minds of all for hours.

But, after all, was it so foreign?

"Inform Prince Sovan," he directed, "that it is our wish that the fleet which departed for Kaol this morning be recalled to cruise to the west of Ptarth."

As the warship, bearing Astok back to the court of his father, turned toward the west, Thuvia of Ptarth, sitting upon the same bench where the Prince of Dusar had affronted her, watched the twinkling lights of the craft growing smaller in the distance. Beside her, in the brilliant light of the nearer moon, sat Carthoris. His eyes were not upon the dim bulk of the battleship, but on the profile of the girl's upturned face.

"Thuvia," he whispered.

The girl turned her eyes toward his. His hand stole out to find hers, but she drew her own gently away.

"Thuvia of Ptarth, I love you!" cried the young warrior. "Tell me that it does not offend."

She shook her head sadly. "The love of Carthoris of Helium," she said simply, "could be naught but an honour to any woman; but you must not speak, my friend, of bestowing upon me that which I may not reciprocate."

The young man got slowly to his feet. His eyes were wide in astonishment. It never had occurred to the Prince of Helium that Thuvia of Ptarth might love another.

"But at Kadabra!" he exclaimed. "And later here at your father's court, what did you do, Thuvia of Ptarth, that might have warned me that you could not return my love?"

"And what did I do, Carthoris of Helium," she returned, "that might lead you to believe that I *did* return it?"

He paused in thought, and then shook his head. "Nothing, Thuvia, that is true; yet I could have sworn you loved me. Indeed, you well knew how near to worship has been my love for you."

"And how might I know it, Carthoris?" she asked innocently. "Did you ever tell me as much? Ever before have words of love for me fallen from your lips?"

"But you *must* have known it!" he exclaimed. "I am like my father—witless in matters of the heart, and of a poor way with women; yet the jewels that strew these royal garden paths—the trees, the flowers, the sward— all must have read the love that has filled my heart since first my eyes were made new by imaging your perfect face and form; so how could you alone have been blind to it?"

"Do the maids of Helium pay court to their men?" asked Thuvia.

"You are playing with me!" exclaimed Carthoris. "Say that you are but playing, and that after all you love me, Thuvia!"

"I cannot tell you that, Carthoris, for I am promised to another."

Her tone was level, but was there not within it the hint of an infinite depth of sadness? Who may say?

"Promised to another?" Carthoris scarcely breathed the words. His face went almost white, and then his head came up as befitted him in whose veins flowed the blood of the overlord of a world.

"Carthoris of Helium wishes you every happiness with the man of your choice," he said. "With——" and then he hesitated, waiting for her to fill in the name.

"Kulan Tith, Jeddak of Kaol," she replied. "My father's friend and Ptarth's most puissant ally."

The young man looked at her intently for a moment before he spoke again.

"You love him, Thuvia of Ptarth?" he asked.

"I am promised to him," she replied simply.

He did not press her. "He is of Barsoom's noblest blood and mightiest fighters," mused Carthoris. "My father's friend and mine—would that it might have been another!" he muttered almost savagely. What the girl thought was hidden by the mask of her expression, which was tinged only by a little shadow of sadness that might have been for Carthoris, herself, or for them both.

Carthoris of Helium did not ask, though he noted it, for his loyalty to Kulan Tith was the loyalty of the blood of John Carter of Virginia for a friend, greater than which could be no loyalty.

He raised a jewel-encrusted bit of the girl's mangificent trappings to his lips.

"To the honour and happiness of Kulan Tith and the priceless jewel that has been bestowed upon him," he said, and though his voice was husky there was the true ring of sincerity in it. "I told you that I loved you, Thuvia, before I knew that you were promised to another. I may not tell you it again, but I am glad that you know it, for there is no dishonour in it either to you or to Kulan Tith or to myself. My love is such that it may embrace as well Kulan Tith—if you love him." There was almost a question in the statement.

"I am promised to him," she replied.

Carthoris backed slowly away. He laid one hand upon his heart, the other upon the pommel of his long-sword.

"These are yours—always," he said. A moment later he had entered the palace, and was gone from the girl's sight.

Had he returned at once he would have found her prone upon the ersite bench, her face buried in her arms. Was she weeping? There was none to see.

Carthoris of Helium had come all unannounced to the court of his father's friend that day. He had come alone in a small flier, sure of the same welcome that always awaited him at Ptarth. As there had been no formality in his coming there was no need of formality in his going.

To Thuvan Dihn he explained that he had been but testing an invention of his own with which his flier was equipped—a clever improvement of the ordinary Martian air compass, which, when set for a certain destination, will remain constantly fixed thereon, making it only necessary to keep a vessel's prow always in the direction of the compass needle to reach any given point upon Barsoom by the shortest route.

Carthoris' improvement upon this consisted of an auxiliary device which steered the craft mechanically in the direction of the compass, and upon arrival directly over the point for which the compass was set, brought the craft to a standstill and lowered it, also automatically, to the ground.

"You readily discern the advantages of this invention," he was saying to Thuvan Dihn, who had accompanied him to the landing-stage upon the palace roof to inspect the compass and bid his young friend farewell.

A dozen officers of the court with several body servants were grouped behind the jeddak and his guest, eager listeners to the conversation—so eager on the part of one of the servants that he was twice rebuked by a noble for his forwardness in pushing himself ahead of his betters to view the intricate mechanism of the wonderful "controlling destination compass," as the thing was called.

"For example," continued Carthoris, "I have an all-night trip before me, as to-night. I set the pointer here upon the right-hand dial which represents the eastern hemisphere of Barsoom, so that the point rests upon the exact latitude and longitude of Helium. Then I start the engine, roll up in my sleeping silks and furs, and with lights burning, race through the air toward Helium, confident that at the appointed hour I shall drop gently toward the landing-stage upon my own palace, whether I am still asleep or no."

"Provided," suggested Thuvan Dihn, "you do not chance to collide with some other night wanderer in the meanwhile."

Cathoris smiled. "No danger of that," he replied. "See here," and he indicated a device at the right of the destination compass. "This is my 'obstruction evader,' as I call it. This visible device is the switch which throws the mechanism on or off. The instrument itself is below deck, geared both to the steering aparatus and the control levers.

"It is quite simple, being nothing more than a radium generator diffusing radio-activity in all directions to a distance of a hundred yards or so from the flier. Should this enveloping force be interrupted in any direction a delicate instrument immediately apprehends the irregularity, at the same time imparting an impulse to a magnetic device which in turn actuates the steering mechanism, diverting the bow of the flier away from the obstacle until the craft's radio-activity sphere is no longer in contact with the obstruction, then she falls once more into her normal course. Should the disturbance approach from the rear, as in case of a faster-moving craft overhauling me, the mechanism actuates the speed control as well as the steering gear, and the flier shoots ahead and either up or down, as the oncoming vessel is upon a lower or higher plane than herself.

"In aggravated cases, that is when the obstructions are many, or of such a nature as to deflect the bow more than forty-five degrees in any direction, or when the craft has reached its destination and dropped to within a hundred yards of the ground, the mechanism brings her to a full stop, at the same time sounding a loud alarm which will instantly awaken the pilot. You see I have anticipated almost every contingency."

Thuvan Dihn smiled his appreciation of the marvellous device. The forward servant pushed almost to the flier's side. His eyes were narrowed to slits.

"All but one," he said.

The nobles looked at him in astonishment, and one of them grasped the fellow none too gently by the shoulder to push him back to his proper place. Carthoris raised his hand.

"Wait," he urged. "Let us hear what the man has to say—no creation of mortal mind is perfect. Perchance he has detected a weakness that it will be well to know at once. Come, my good fellow, and what may be the one contingency I have overlooked?"

As he spoke Carthoris observed the servant closely for the first time. He saw a man of giant stature and handsome, as are all those of the race of Martian red men; but the fellow's lips were thin and cruel, and across one cheek was the faint, white line of a sword-cut from the right temple to the corner of the mouth.

"Come," urged the Prince of Helium. "Speak!"

The man hesitated. It was evident that he regretted the temerity that had made him the centre of interested observation. But at last, seeing no alternative, he spoke.

"It might be tampered with," he said, "by an enemy."

Carthoris drew a small key from his leathern pocket-pouch.

"Look at this," he said, handing it to the man. "If you know aught of locks, you will know that the mechanism which this unlooses is beyond the cunning of a picker of locks. It guards the vitals of the instrument from crafty tampering. Without it an enemy must half wreck the device to reach its heart, leaving his handiwork apparent to the most casual observer."

The servant took the key, glanced at it shrewdly, and then as he made to return it to Carthoris dropped it upon the marble flagging. Turning to look for it he planted the sole of his sandal full upon the glittering object. For an instant he bore all his weight upon the foot that covered the key, then he stepped back and with an exclamation as of pleasure that he had found it, stooped, recovered it, and returned it to the Heliumite. Then he dropped back to his station behind the nobles and was forgotten.

A moment later Carthoris had made his adieux to Thuvan Dihn and his nobles, and with lights twinkling had risen into the star-shot void of the Martian night.

CHAPTER II

SLAVERY

As THE RULER of Ptarth, followed by his courtiers, descended from the landing-stage above the palace, the servants dropped into their places in the rear of their royal or noble masters, and behind the others one lingered to the last. Then quickly stooping he snatched the sandal from his right foot, slipping it into his pocket-pouch.

When the party had come to the lower levels, and the jeddak had dispersed them by a sign, none noticed that the forward fellow who had drawn so much attention to himself before the Prince of Helium departed, was no longer among the other servants.

To whose retinue he had been attached none had thought to inquire, for the followers of a Martian noble are many, coming and going at the whim of their master, so that a new face is scarcely ever questioned, as the fact that a man has passed within the palace walls is considered proof positive that his loyalty to the jeddak is beyond question, so rigid is the examination of each who seeks service with the nobles of the court.

A good rule that, and only relaxed by courtesy in favour of the retinue of visiting royalty from a friendly foreign power.

It was late in the morning of the next day that a giant serving man in the harness of the house of a great Ptarth noble passed out ino the city from the palace gates. Along one broad avenue and then another he strode briskly until he had passed beyond the district of the nobles and had come to the place of shops. Here he sought a pretentious building that rose spire-like toward the heavens, its outer walls elaborately wrought with delicate carvings and intricate mosaics.

It was the Palace of Peace in which were housed the representatives of the foreign powers, or rather in which were located their embassies; for the ministers themselves dwelt in gorgeous palaces within the district occupied by the nobles.

Here the man sought the embassy of Dusar. A clerk arose questioningly as he entered, and at his request to have a word with the minister asked his credentials. The visitor slipped a plain metal armlet from above his elbow, and pointing to an inscription upon its inner surface, whispered a word or two to the clerk.

The latter's eyes went wide, and his attitude turned at once to one of deference. He bowed the stranger to a seat, and hastened to an inner room with the armlet in his hand. A moment later he reappeared and conducted the caller into the presence of the minister.

For a long time the two were closeted together, and when at last the giant serving man emerged from the inner office his expression was cast in a smile of sinister satisfaction. From the Palace of Peace he hurried directly to the palace of the Dusarian minister.

That night two swift fliers left the same palace top. One sped its rapid course toward Helium; the other——

Thuvia of Ptarth strolled in the gardens of her father's palace, as was her nightly custom before retiring. Her silks and furs were drawn about her, for the air of Mars is chill after the sun has taken his quick plunge beneath the planet's western verge.

The girl's thoughts wandered from her impending nuptials, that would make her empress of Kaol, to the person of the trim young Heliumite who had laid his heart at her feet the preceding day.

Whether it was pity or regret that saddened her expression as she gazed toward the southern heavens where she had watched the lights of his flier disappear the previous night, it would be difficult to say.

So, too, is it impossible to conjecture just what her emotions may have been as she discerned the lights of a flier speeding rapidly out of the distance from that very direction, as though impelled toward her garden by the very intensity of the princess' thoughts.

She saw it circle lower above the palace until she was positive that it but hovered in preparation for a landing.

Presently the powerful rays of its searchlight shot downward from the bow. They fell upon the landing-stage for a brief instant, revealing the figures of the Ptarthian guard, picking into brilliant points of fire the gems upon their gorgeous harnesses.

Then the blazing eye swept onward across the burnished domes and graceful minarets, down into court and park and garden to pause at last upon the ersite bench and the girl standing there beside it, her face upturned full toward the flier.

For but an instant the searchlight halted upon Thuvia of Ptarth, then it was extinguished as suddenly as it had come to life. The flier passed on above her to disappear beyond a grove of lofty skeel trees that grew within the palace grounds.

The girl stood for some time as it had left her, except that her head was bent and her eyes downcast in thought.

Who but Carthoris could it have been? She tried to feel anger that he should have returned thus, spying upon her; but she found it difficult to be angry with the young prince of Helium.

What mad caprice could have induced him so to transgress the etiquette of nations? For lesser things great powers had gone to war.

The princess in her was shocked and angered—but what of the girl!

And the guard—what of them? Evidently they, too, had been so much surprised by the unprecedented action of the stranger that they had not even challenged; but that they had no thought to let the thing go unnoticed was quickly evidenced by the skirring of motors upon the landing-stage and the quick shooting airward of a long-lined patrol boat.

Thuvia watched it dart swiftly eastward. So, too, did other eyes watch.

Within the dense shadows of the skeel grove, in a wide avenue beneath o'erspreading foliage, a flier hung a dozen feet above the ground. From its deck keen eyes watched the far-fanning searchlight of the patrol boat. No light shone from the enshadowed craft. Upon its desk was the silence of the tomb. Its crew of a half-dozen red warriors watched the lights of the patrol boat diminishing in the distance.

"The intellects of our ancestors are with us to-night," said one in a low tone.

"No plan ever carried better," returned another. "They did precisely as the prince foretold."

He who had first spoken turned toward the man who squatted before the control board.

"Now!" he whispered. There was no other order given. Every man upon the craft had evidently been well schooled in each detail of that night's work. Silently the dark hull crept beneath the cathedral arches of the dark and silent grove.

Thuvia of Ptarth, gazing toward the east, saw the blacker blot against the blackness of the trees as the craft topped the buttressed garden wall. She saw the dim bulk incline gently downward toward the scarlet sward of the garden.

She knew that men came not thus with honourable intent. Yet she did not cry aloud to alarm the near-by guardsmen, nor did she flee to the safety of the palace.

Why?

I can see her shrug her shapely shoulders in reply as she voices the age-old, universal answer of the woman: Because!

Scarce had the flier touched the ground when four men leaped from its deck. They ran forward toward the girl.

Still she made no sign of alarm, standing as though hypnotized. Or could it have been as one who awaited a welcome visitor?

Not until they were quite close to her did she move. Then the nearer moon, rising above the surrounding foliage, touched their faces, lighting all with the brilliancy of her silver rays.

Thurvia of Ptarth saw only strangers—warriors in the harness of Dusar. Now she took fright, but too late!

Before she could voice but a single cry, rough hands seized her. A heavy silken scarf was wound about her head. She was lifted in strong arms and borne to the deck of the flier. There was the sudden whirl of propellers, the rushing of air against her body, and, from far beneath the shouting and the challenge from the guard.

Racing toward the south another flier sped toward Helium. In its cabin a tall red man bent over the soft sole of an upturned sandal. With delicate instruments he measured the faint imprint of a small object with appeared there. Upon a pad beside him was the outline of a key, and here he noted the results of his measurements.

A smile played upon his lips as he completed his task and turned to one who waited at the opposite side of the table.

"The man is a genius," he remarked.

"Only a genius could have evolved such a lock as this is designed to spring. Here, take the sketch, Larok, and give all thine own genius full and unfettered freedom in reproducing it in metal."

The warrior-artificer bowed. "Man builds naught," he said, "that man may not destroy." Then he left the cabin with the sketch.

As dawn broke upon the lofty towers which mark the twin cities of Helium—the scarlet tower of one and the yellow tower of its sister—a flier floated lazily out of the north.

Upon its bow was emblazoned the signia of a lesser noble of a far city of the empire of Helium. Its leisurely approach and the evident confidence with which it moved across the city aroused no suspicion in the minds of the sleepy guard. Their round of duty nearly done, they had little thought beyond the coming of those who were to relieve them.

Peace reigned throughout Helium. Stagnant, emasculating peace. Helium had no enemies. There was naught to fear.

Without haste the nearest air patrol swung sluggishly about and approached the stranger. At easy speaking distance the officer upon her deck hailed the incoming craft.

The cheery "Kaor!" and the plausible explanation that the owner had come from distant parts for a few days of pleasure in gay Helium sufficed. The air-patrol boat she off, passing again upon its way. The stranger continued toward a public landing-stage, where she dropped into the ways and came to rest.

At about the same time a warrior entered her cabin.

"It is done, Vas Kor," he said, handing a small metal key to the tall noble who had just risen from his sleeping silks and furs.

"Good!" exclaimed the latter. "You must have worked upon it all during the night, Larok."

The warrior nodded.

"Now fetch me the Heliumetic metal you wrought some days since," commanded Vas Kor.

This done, the warrior assisted his master to replace the handsome jewelled metal of his harness with the plainer ornaments of an ordinary fighting man of Helium, and with the insignia of the same house that appeared upon the bow of the flier.

Vas Kor breakfasted on board. Then he emerged upon the aerial dock, entered an elevator, and was borne quickly to the street below, where he was soon engulfed by the early morning throng of workers hastening to their daily duties.

Among them his warrior trappings were no more remarkable than is a pair of trousers upon Broadway. All Martian men are warriors, save those physically unable to bear arms. The tradesman and his clerk clank with their martial trappings as they pursue their vocations. The schoolboy, coming into the world, as he does, almost adult from the snowy shell that has encompassed his development for five long years, knows so little of life without a sword at his hip that he would feel the same discomfiture at going abroad unarmed that an Earth boy would experience in walking the streets knickerbockerless.

Vas Kor's destination lay in Greater Helium, which lies some seventy-five miles across the level plain from Lesser Helium. He had landed at the latter city because the air patrol is less suspicious and alert than that above the larger metropolis where lies the palace of the jeddak.

As he moved with the throng in the parklike canyon of the thoroughfare the life of an awakening Martian city was in evidence about him. Houses, raised high upon their slender metal columns for the night were dropping gently toward the ground. Among the flowers upon the scarlet sward which lies about the buildings children were already playing, and comely women laughing and chatting with their neighbours as they culled gorgeous blossoms for the vases within doors.

The pleasant "kàor" of the Barsoomian greeting fell continually upon the ears of the stranger as friends and neighbours took up the duties of a new day.

The district in which he had landed was residential—a district of merchants of the more prosperous sort. Everywhere were evidences of luxury and wealth. Slaves appeared upon every housetop with gorgeous silks and costly furs, laying them in the sun for airing. Jewel-encrusted women lolled even thus early upon the carven balconies before their sleeping apartments. Later in the day they would repair to the roofs when the slaves had arranged couches and pitched silken canopies to shade them from the sun.

Strains of inspiring music broke pleasantly from open windows, for the Martians have solved the problem of attuning the nerves pleasantly to the sudden transition from sleep to waking that proves so difficult a thing for most Earth folk.

Above him raced the long, light passenger fliers, plying, each in its proper plane, between the numerous landing-stages for internal passenger traffic. Landing-stages that tower high into the heavens are for the great international passenger liners. Freighters have other landing-stages at various lower levels, to within a couple of hundred feet of the ground; nor dare any flier rise or drop from one plane to another except in certain restricted districts where horizontal traffic is forbidden.

Along the close-cropped sward which paves the avenue ground fliers were moving in continuous lines in opposite directions. For the greater part they skimmed along the surface of the sward, soaring gracefully into the air at times to pass over a slower-going driver ahead, or at intersections, where the north and south traffic has the right of way and the east and west must rise above it.

From private hangars upon many a roof top fliers were darting into the line of traffic. Gay farewells and parting admonitions mingled with the whirring of motors and the subdued noises of the city.

Yet with all the swift movement and the countless thousands rushing hither and thither, the predominant suggestion was that of luxurious ease and soft noiselessness.

Martians dislike harsh, discordant clamour. The only loud noises they can abide are the martial sounds of war, the clash of arms, the collision of two mighty dreadnoughts of the air. To them there is no sweeter music than this.

At the intersection of two broad avenues Vas Kor descended from the street level to one of the great pneumatic stations of the city. Here he paid before a little wicket the fare to his destination with a couple of the dull, oval coins of Helium.

Beyond the gatekeeper he came to a slowly moving line of what to Earthly eyes would have appeared to be conical-nosed, eight-foot projectiles for some giant gun. In slow procession the things moved in single file along a grooved track. A half dozen attendants assisted passengers to enter, or directed these carriers to their proper destination.

Vas Kor approached one that was empty. Upon its nose was a dial and a pointer. He set the pointer for a certain station in Greater Helium, raised the arched lid of the thing, stepped in and lay down upon the upholstered bottom. An attendant closed the lid, which locked with a little click, and the carrier continued its slow way.

Presently it switched itself automatically to another track, to enter, a moment later, one of the series of dark-mouthed tubes.

The instant that its entire length was within the black aperture it sprang forward with the speed of a rifle ball. There was an instant of whizzing—a soft, though sudden, stop, and slowly the carrier emerged upon another platform, another attendant raised the lid and Vas Kor stepped out at the station beneath the centre of Greater Helium, seventy-five miles from the point at which he had embarked.

Here he sought the street level, stepping immediately into a waiting ground flier. He spoke no word to the slave sitting in the driver's seat. It was evident that he had been expected, and that the fellow had received his instructions before his coming.

Scarcely had Vas Kor taken his seat when the flier went quickly into the fast-moving procession, turning presently from the broad and crowded avenue into a less congested street. Presently it left the thronged district behind to enter a section of small shops, where it stopped before the entrance to one which bore the sign of a dealer in foreign silks.

Vas Kor entered the low-ceiling room. A man at the

far end motioned him toward an inner apartment, giving no further sign of recognition until he had passed in after the caller and closed the door.

Then he faced his visitor, saluting deferentially.

"Most noble——" he commenced, but Vas Kor silenced him with a gesture.

"No formalities," he said. "We must forget that I am aught other than your slave. If all has been as carefully carried out as it has been planned, we have no time to waste. Instead we should be upon our way to the slave market. Are you ready?"

The merchant nodded, and, turning to a great chest, produced the unemblazoned trappings of a slave. These Vas Kor immediately donned. Then the two passed from the shop through a rear door, traversed a winding alley to an avenue beyond, where they entered a flier which awaited them.

Five minutes later the merchant was leading his slave to the public market, where a great concourse of people filled the great open space in the centre of which stood the slave block.

The crowds were enormous to-day, for Carthoris, Prince of Helium, was to be the principal bidder.

One by one the masters mounted the rostrum beside the slave block upon which stood their chattels. Briefly and clearly each recounted the virtues of his particular offering.

When all were done, the major-domo of the Prince of Helium recalled to the block such as had favourably impressed him. For such he had made a fair offer.

There was little haggling as to price, and none at all when Vas Kor was placed upon the block. His merchant-master accepted the first offer that was made for him, and thus a Dusarian noble entered the household of Carthoris.

CHAPTER III

TREACHERY

THE DAY FOLLOWING the coming of Vas Kor to the palace of the Prince of Helium great excitement reigned throughout the twin cities, reaching its climax in the palace of Carthoris. Word had come of the abduction of Thuvia of Ptarth from her father's court, and with it the veiled hint that the Prince of Helium might be suspected of considerable knowledge of the act and the whereabouts of the princess.

In the council chamber of John Carter, Warlord of Mars, was Tardos Mors, Jeddak of Helium; Mors Kajak, his son, Jed of Lesser Helium; Carthoris, and a score of the great nobles of the empire.

"There must be no war between Ptarth and Helium, my son," said John Carter. "That you are innocent of the charge that has been placed against you by insinuation, we well know; but Thuvan Dihn must know it well, too.

"There is but one who may convince him, and that one be you. You must hasten at once to the court of Ptarth, and by your presence there as well as by your words assure him that his suspicions are groundless. Bear with you the authority of the Warlord of Barsoom, and of the Jeddak of Helium to offer every resource of the allied powers to assist Thuvan Dihn to recover his daughter and punish her abductors, whomsoever they may be.

"Go! I know that I do not need to urge upon you the necessity for haste."

Carthoris left the council chamber, and hastened to his palace.

Here slaves were busy in a moment setting things to rights for the departure of their master. Several worked about the swift flier that would bear the Prince of Helium rapidly toward Ptarth.

At last all was done. But two armed slaves remained on guard. The setting sun hung low above the horizon. In a moment darkness would envelop all.

One of the guardsmen, a giant of a fellow across whose right cheek there ran a thin scar from temple to mouth, approached his companion. His gaze was directed beyond and above his comrade. When he had come quite close he spoke.

"What strange craft is that?" he asked.

The other turned about quickly to gaze heavenward. Scarce was his back turned toward the giant than the short-sword of the latter was plunged beneath his left shoulder blade, straight through his heart.

Voiceless, the soldier sank in his tracks—stone dead. Quickly the murderer dragged the corpse into the black shadows within the hangar. Then he returned to the flier.

Drawing a cunningly wrought key from his pocket-pouch, he removed the cover of the right-hand dial of the controlling destination compass. For a moment he studied the construction of the mechanism beneath. Then he returned the dial to its place, set the pointer, and re-moved it again to note the resultant change in the position of the parts affected by the act.

A smile crossed his lips. With a pair of cutters he snipped off the projection which extended through the dial from the external pointer—now the latter might be moved to any point upon the dial without affecting the mechanism below. In other words, the eastern hemisphere dial was useless.

Now he turned his attention to the western dial. This he set upon a certain point. Afterward he removed the cover of this dial also, and with keen tool cut the steel finger from the under side of the pointer.

As quickly as possible he replaced the second dial cover, and resumed his place on guard. To all intents and purposes the compass was as efficient as before; but, as a matter of fact, the moving of the pointers upon the dials resulted now in no corresponding shift of the mechanism beneath—and the device was set, immovably, upon a destination of the slave's own choosing.

Presently came Carthoris, accompanied by but a handful of his gentlemen. He cast but a casual glance upon the single slave who stood guard. The fellow's thin, cruel lips, and the sword-cut that ran from temple to mouth aroused the suggestion of an unpleasant memory within him. He wondered where Saran Tal had found the man—then the matter faded from his thoughts, and in another moment the Prince of Helium was laughing and chatting with his companions, though below the surface his heart was cold with dread, for what contingencies confronted Thuvia of Ptarth he could not even guess.

First to his mind, naturally, had sprung the thought that Astok of Dusar had stolen the fair Ptarthian; but almost simultaneously with the report of the abduction had come news of the great fêtes at Dusar in honour of the return of the jeddak's son to the court of his father.

It could not have been he, thought Carthoris, for on the very night that Thuvia was taken Astok had been in Dusar, and yet——

He entered the flier, exchanging casual remarks with his companions as he unlocked the mechanism of the compass and set the pointer upon the capital city of Ptarth.

With a word of farewell he touched the button which controlled the repulsive rays, and as the flier rose lightly into the air, the engine purred in answer to the touch of his finger upon a second button, the propellers whirred as his hand drew back the speed lever, and Carthoris,

Prince of Helium, was off into the gorgeous Martian night beneath the hurtling moons and the million stars.

Scarce had the flier found its speed ere the man, wrapping his sleeping silks and furs about him, stretched at full length upon the narrow deck to sleep.

But sleep did not come at once at his bidding.

Instead, his thoughts ran riot in his brain, driving sleep away. He recalled the words of Thuvia of Ptarth, words that had half assured him that she loved him; for when he had asked her if she loved Kulan Tith, she had answered only that she was promised to him.

Now he saw that her reply was open to more than a single construction. It might, of course, mean that she did not love Kulan Tith; and so, by inference, be taken to mean that she loved another.

But what assurance was there that the other was Carthoris of Helium?

The more he thought upon it the more positive he became that not only was there no assurance in her words that she loved him, but none either in any act of hers. No, the fact was, she did not love him. She loved another. She had not been abducted—she had fled willingly with her lover.

With such pleasant thoughts filling him alternately with despair and rage, Carthoris at last dropped into the sleep of utter mental exhaustion.

The breaking of the sudden dawn found him still asleep. His flier was rushing swiftly above a barren, ochre plain—he world-old bottom of a long-dead Martian sea.

In the distance rose low hills. Toward these the craft was headed. As it approached them, a great promontory might have been seen from its deck, stretching out into what had once been a mighty ocean, and circling back once more to enclose the forgotten harbour of a forgotten city, which still stretched back from its deserted quays, an imposing pile of wondrous architecture of a long-dead past.

The countless dismal windows, vacant and forlorn, stared, sightless, from their marble walls; the whole sad city taking on the semblance of scattered mounds of dead men's sun-bleached skulls—the casements having the appearance of eyeless sockets, the portals, grinning jaws.

Closer came the flier, but now its speed was diminishing—yet this was not Ptarth.

Above the central plaza it stopped, slowly settling Marsward. Within a hundred yards of the ground it came to rest, floating gently in the light air, and at the same instant an alarm sounded at the sleeper's ear.

Carthoris sprang to his feet. Below him he looked to see the teeming metropolis of Ptarth. Beside him, already, there should have been an air patrol.

He gazed about in bewildered astonishment. There indeed was a great city, but it was not Ptarth. No multitudes surged through its broad avenues. No signs of life broke the dead monotony of its deserted roof tops. No gorgeous silks, no priceless furs lent life and colour to the cold marble and the gleaming ersite.

No patrol boat lay ready with its familiar challenge. Silent and empty lay the great city—empty and silent the surrounding air.

What had happened?

Carthoris examined the dial of his compass. The pointer was set upon Ptarth. Could the creature of his genius have thus betrayed him? He would not believe it.

Quickly he unlocked the cover, turning it back upon its hinge. A single glance showed him the truth, or at least a part of it—the steel projection that communicated the movement of the pointer upon the dial to the heart of the mechanism beneath had been severed.

Who could have done the thing—and why?

Carthoris could not hazard even a faint guess. But the thing now was to learn in what portion of the world he was, and then take up his interrupted journey once more.

If it had been the purpose of some enemy to delay him, he had succeeded well, thought Carthoris, as he unlocked the cover of the second dial the first having shown that its pointer had not been set at all.

Beneath the second dial he found the steel pin severed as in the other, but the controlling mechanism had first been set for a point upon the western hemisphere.

He had just time to judge his location roughly at some place south-west of Helium, and at a considerable distance from the twin cities, when he was startled by a woman's scream beneath him.

Leaning over the side of the flier, he saw what appeared to be a red woman being dragged across the plaza by a huge, green warrior—one of those fierce, cruel denizens of the dead sea-bottoms and deserted cities of dying Mars.

Carthoris waited to see no more. Reaching for the control board, he sent his craft racing plummet-like toward the ground.

The green man was hurrying his captive toward a huge thoat that browsed upon the ochre vegetation of the once scarlet-gorgeous plaza. At the same instant a dozen red warriors leaped from the entrance of a near-by ersite palace, pursuing the abductor with naked swords and shouts of rageful warning.

Once the woman turned her face upward toward the falling flier, and in the single swift glance Carthoris saw that it was Thuvia of Ptarth!

CHAPTER IV

A GREEN MAN'S CAPTIVE

WHEN THE LIGHT of day broke upon the little craft to whose deck the Princess of Ptarth had been snatched from her father's garden, Thuvia saw that the night had wrought a change in her abductors.

No longer did their trappings gleam with the metal of Dusar, but instead there was emblazoned there the insignia of the Prince of Helium.

The girl felt renewed hope, for she could not believe that in the heart of Carthoris could lie intent to harm her.

She spoke to the warrior squatting before the control board.

"Last night you wore the trappings of a Dusarian," she said. "Now your metal is that of Helium. What means it?"

The man looked at her with a grin.

"The Prince of Helium is no fool," he said.

Just then an officer emerged from the tiny cabin. He reprimanded the warrior for conversing with the prisoner, nor would he himself reply to any of her inquiries.

No harm was offered her during the journey, and so they came at last to their destination with the girl no wiser as to her abductors or their purpose than at first.

Here the flier settled slowly into the plaza of one of those mute monuments of Mars' dead and forgotten past

—the deserted cities that fringe the sad ochre sea-bottoms where once rolled the mighty floods upon whose bosoms moved the maritime commerce of the peoples that are gone for ever.

Thuvia of Ptarth was no stranger to such places. During her wanderings in search of the River Iss, that time she had set out upon what, for countless ages, had been the last, long pilgrimage of Martians, toward the Valley Dor, where lies the Lost Sea of Korus, she had encountered several of these sad reminders of the greatness and the glory of ancient Barsoom.

And again, during her flight from the temples of the Holy Therns with Tars Tarkas, Jeddak of Thark, she had seen them, with their weird and ghostly inmates, the great white apes of Barsoom.

She knew, too, that many of them were used now by the nomadic tribes of green men, but that among them all was no city that the red men did not shun, for without exception they stood amidst vast, waterless tracts, unsuited for the continued sustenance of the dominant race of Martians.

Why, then, should they be bringing her to such a place? There was but a single answer. Such was the nature of their work that they must needs seek the seclusion that a dead city afforded. The girl trembled at thought of her plight.

For two days her captors kept her within a huge palace that even in decay reflected the splendour of the age which its youth had known.

Just before dawn on the third day she had been aroused by the voices of two of her abductors.

"He should be here by dawn," one was saying. "Have her in readiness upon the plaza—else he will never land. The moment he finds that he is in a strange country he will turn about—methinks the prince's plan is weak in this one spot."

"There was no other way," replied the other. "It is wondrous work to get them both here at all, and even if we do not succeed in luring him to the ground, we shall have accomplished much."

Just then the speaker caught the eyes of Thuvia upon him, revealed by the quick-moving patch of light cast by Thuvia in her mad race through the heavens.

With a quick sign to the other, he ceased speaking, and advancing toward the girl, motioned her to rise. Then he led her out into the night toward the centre of the great plaza.

"Stand here," he commanded, "until we come for you. We shall be watching, and should you attempt to escape it will go ill with you—much worse than death. Such are the prince's orders."

Then he turned and retraced his steps toward the palace, leaving her alone in the midst of the unseen terrors of the haunted city, for in truth these places are haunted in the belief of many Martians who still cling to an ancient superstition which teaches that the spirits of Holy Therns who die before their allotted one thousand years, pass, on occasions, into the bodies of the great white apes.

To Thuvia, however, the real danger of attack by one of these ferocious, manlike beasts was quite sufficient. She no longer believed in the weird soul transmigration that the therns had taught her before she was rescued from their clutches by John Carter; but she well knew the horrid fate that awaited her should one of the terrible beasts chance to spy her during its nocturnal prowlings.

What was that?

Surely she could not be mistaken. Something had moved, stealthily, in the shadow of one of the great monoliths that line the avenue where it entered the plaza opposite her!

Thar Ban, jed among the hordes of Torquas, rode swiftly across the ochre vegetation of the dead sea-bottom toward the ruins of ancient Aaanthor.

He had ridden far that night, and fast, for he had but

come from the despoiling of the incubator of a neigh-
bouring green horde with which the hordes of Torquas
were perpetually warring.

His giant thoat was far from jaded, yet it would be
well, thought Thar Ban, to permit him to graze upon
the ochre moss which grows to greater height within the
protected courtyards of deserted cities, where the soil is
richer than on the sea-bottoms, and the plants partly
shaded from the sun during the cloudless Martian day.

Within the tiny stems of this dry-seeming plant is
sufficient moisture for the needs of the huge bodies of
the mighty thoats, which can exist for months without
water, and for days without even the slight moisture
which the ochre moss contains.

As Thar Ban rode noiselessly up the broad avenue
which leads from the quays of Aaanthor to the great
central plaza, he and his mount might have been mistaken for spectres from a world of dreams, so grotesque
the man and beast, so soundless the great thoat's padded,
nailless feet upon the moss-grown flagging of the ancient
pavement.

The man was a splendid specimen of his race. Fully
fifteen feet towered his great height from sole to pate.
The moonlight glistened against his glossy green hide,
sparkling the jewels of his heavy harness and the ornaments that weighted his four muscular arms, while the
upcurving tusks that protruded from his lower jaw
gleamed white and terrible.

At the side of his thoat were slung his long radium
rifle and his great, forty-foot, metal-shod spear, while
from his own harness depended his long-sword and his
short-sword, as well as his lesser weapons.

His protruding eyes and antennæ-like ears were turning constantly hither and thither, for Thar Ban was yet
in the country of the enemy, and, too, there was always
the menace of the great white apes, which, John Carter
was wont to say, are the only creatures that can arouse
in the breasts of these fierce denizens of the dead sea-
bottoms even the remotest semblance of fear.

As the rider neared the plaza, he reined suddenly in. His slender, tubular ears pointed rigidly forward. An unwonted sound had reached them. Voices! And where there were voices, outside of Torquas, there, too, were enemies. All the world of wide Barsoom contained naught but enemies for the fierce Torquasians.

Thar Ban dismounted. Keeping in the shadows of the great monoliths that line the Avenue of Quays of sleeping Aaanthor, he approached the plaza. Directly behind him, as a hound at heel, came the slate-grey thoat, his white belly shadowed by his barrel, his vivid yellow feet merging into the yellow of the moss beneath them.

In the centre of the plaza Thar Ban saw the figure of a red woman. A red warrior was conversing with her. Now the man turned and retraced his steps toward the palace at the opposite side of the plaza.

Thar Ban watched until he had disappeared within the yawning portal. Here was a captive worth having! Seldom did a female of their hereditary enemies fall to the lot of a green man. Thar Ban licked his thin lips.

Thuvia of Ptarth watched the shadow behind the monolith at the opening to the avenue opposite her. She hoped that it might be but the figment of an overwrought imagination.

But no! Now, clearly and distinctly, she saw it move. It came from behind the screening shelter of the ersite shaft.

The sudden light of the rising sun fell upon it. The girl trembled. The *thing* was a huge green warrior!

Swiftly it sprang toward her. She screamed and tried to flee; but she had scarce turned toward the palace when a giant hand fell upon her arm, she was whirled about, and half dragged, half carried toward a huge thoat that was slowly grazing out of the avenue's mouth on to the ochre moss of the plaza.

At the same instant she turned her face upward toward the whirring sound of something above her, and there she saw a swift flier dropping toward her, the head and shoulders of a man leaning far over the side; but the man's features were deeply shadowed, so that she did not recognize them.

Now from behind her came the shouts of her red abductors. They were racing madly after him who dared to steal what they already had stolen.

As Thar Ban reached the side of his mount he snatched his long radium rifle from its boot, and, wheeling, poured three shots into the oncoming red men.

Such is the uncanny marksmanship of these Martian savages that three red warriors dropped in their tracks as three projectiles exploded in their vitals.

The others halted, nor did they dare return the fire for fear of wounding the girl.

Then Thar Ban vaulted to the back of this thoat, Thuvia of Ptarth still in his arms, and with a savage cry of triumph disappeared down the black canyon of the Avenue of Quays between the sullen palaces of forgotten Aaanthor.

Carthoris' flier had not touched the ground before he had sprung from its deck to race after the swift thoat, whose eight long legs were sending it down the avenue at the rate of an express train; but the men of Dusar who still remained alive had no mind to permit so valuable a capture to escape them.

They had lost the girl. That would be a difficult thing to explain to Astok; but some leniency might be expected could they carry the Prince of Helium to their master instead.

So the three who remained set upon Carthoris with their long-swords, crying to him to surrender; but they might as successfully have cried aloud to Thuria to cease her mad hurtling through the Barsoomian sky, for Carthoris of Helium was a true son of the Warlord of Mars and his incomparable Dejah Thoris.

Carthoris' long-sword had been already in his hand as he leaped from the deck of the flier, so the instant that he realized the menace of the three red warriors, he wheeled to face them, meeting their onslaught as only John Carter himself might have done.

So swift his sword, so mighty and agile his half-earthly muscles, that one of his opponents was down, crimsoning the ochre moss with his life-blood, when he had scarce made a single pass at Carthoris.

Now the two remaining Dusarians rushed simultaneously upon the Heliumite. Three long-swords clashed and sparkled in the moonlight, until the great white apes, roused from their slumbers, crept to the lowering windows of the dead city to view the bloody scene beneath them.

Thrice was Carthoris touched, so that the red blood ran down his face, blinding him and dyeing his broad chest. With his free hand he wiped the gore from his eyes, and with the fighting smile of his father touching his lips, leaped upon his antagonists with renewed fury.

A single cut of his heavy sword severed the head of one of them, and then the other, backing away clear of that point of death, turned and fled toward the palace at his back.

Carthoris made no step to pursue. He had other concern than the meting of even well-deserved punishment to strange men who masqueraded in the metal of his own house, for he had seen that these men were tricked out in the insignia that marked his personal followers.

Turning quickly toward his flier, he was soon rising from the plaza in pursuit of Thar Ban.

The red warrior whom he had put to flight turned in the entrance to the palace, and, seeing Carthoris' intent, snatched a rifle from those that he and his fellows had left leaning against the wall as they had rushed out with drawn swords to prevent the theft of their prisoner.

Few red men are good shots, for the sword is their chosen weapon; so now as the Dusarian drew bead upon the rising flier, and touched the button upon his rifle's stock, it was more to chance than proficiency that he owed the partial success of his aim.

The projectile grazed the flier's side, the opaque coating breaking sufficiently to permit daylight to strike in upon the powder phial within the bullet's nose. There was a sharp explosion. Carthoris felt his craft reel drunkenly beneath him, and the engine stopped.

The momentum the air boat had gained carried her on over the city toward the sea-bottom beyond.

The red warrior in the plaza fired several more shots, none of which scored. Then a lofty minaret shut the drifting quarry from his view.

In the distance before him Carthoris could see the green warrior bearing Thuvia of Ptarth away upon his mighty thoat. The direction of his flight was toward the north-west of Aaanthor, where lay a mountainous country little known to red men.

The Heliumite now gave his attention to his injured craft. A close examination revealed the fact that one of the buoyancy tanks had been punctured, but the engine itself was uninjured.

A splinter from the projectile had damaged one of the control levers beyond the possibility of repair outside a machine shop; but after considerable tinkering, Carthoris was able to propel his wounded flier at low speed, a rate which could not approach the rapid gait of the thoat, whose eight long, powerful legs carried it over the ochre vegetation of the dead sea-bottom at terrific speed.

The Prince of Helium chafed and fretted at the slowness of his pursuit, yet he was thankful that the damage was no worse, for now he could at least move more rapidly than on foot.

But even this meagre satisfaction was soon to be denied him, for presently the flier commenced to sag toward the port and by the bow. The damage to the buoyancy tanks had evidently been more grievous than he had at first believed.

All the balance of that long day Carthoris crawled erratically through the still air, the bow of the flier sinking lower and lower, and the list to port becoming more and more alarming, until at last, near dark, he was floating almost bowdown, his harness buckled to a heavy deck ring to keep him from being precipitated to the ground below.

His forward movement was now confined to a slow drifting with the gentle breeze that blew out of the south-east, and when this died down with the setting of the sun, he let the flier sink gently to the mossy carpet beneath.

Far before him loomed the mountains toward which the green man had been fleeing when last he had seen him, and with dogged resolution the son of John Carter, endowed with the indomitable will of his mighty sire, took up the pursuit on foot.

All that night he forged ahead until, with the dawning of a new day, he entered the low foothills that guard the approach to the fastness of the mountains of Torquas.

Rugged, granitic walls towered before him. Nowhere could he discern an opening through the formidable barrier; yet somewhere into this inhospitable world of stone the green warrior had borne the woman of the red man's heart's desire.

Across the yielding moss of the sea-bottom there had been no spoor to follow, for the soft pads of the thoat but pressed down in his swift passage the resilient vegetation which sprang up again behind his fleeting feet, leaving no sign.

But here in the hills, where loose rock occasionally strewed the way; where black loam and wild flowers partially replaced the sombre monotony of the waste places of the lowlands, Carthoris hoped to find some sign that would lead him in the right direction.

Yet, search as he would, the baffling mystery of the trail seemed likely to remain for ever unsolved.

It was drawing toward the day's close once more when the keen eyes of the Heliumite discerned the tawny yellow of a sleek hide moving among the boulders several hundred yards to his left.

Crouching quickly behind a large rock, Carthoris watched the thing before him. It was a huge banth, one of those savage Barsoomian lions that roam the desolate hills of the dying planet.

The creature's nose was close to the ground. It was evident that he was following the spoor of meat by scent.

As Carthoris watched him, a great hope leaped into the man's heart. Here, possibly, might lie the solution to the mystery he had been endeavouring to solve. This hungry carnivore, keen always for the flesh of man, might even now be trailing the two whom Carthoris sought.

Cautiously the youth crept out upon the trail of the man-eater. Along the foot of the perpendicular cliff the creature moved, sniffing at the invisible spoor, and now and then emitting the low moan of the hunting banth.

Carthoris had followed the creature for but a few minutes when it disappeared as suddenly and mysteriously as though dissolved into thin air.

The man leaped to his feet. Not again was he to be cheated as the man had cheated him. He sprang forward at a reckless pace to the spot at which he last had seen the great, skulking brute.

Before him loomed the sheer cliff, its face unbroken by any aperture into which the huge banth might have wormed its great carcass. Beside him was a small, flat boulder, not larger than the deck of a ten-man flier, nor standing to a greater height than twice his own stature.

Perhaps the banth was in hiding behind this? The brute might have discovered the man upon his trail, and even now be lying in wait for his easy prey.

Cautiously, with drawn long-sword, Carthoris crept around the corner of the rock. There was no banth there, but something which surprised him infinitely more than would the presence of twenty banths.

Before him yawned the mouth of a dark cave leading downward into the ground. Through this the banth must have disappeared. Was it his lair? Within its dark and forbidding interior might there not lurk not one but many of the fearsome creatures?

Carthoris did not know, nor, with the thought that had

been spurring him onward upon the trail of the creature uppermost in his mind, did he much care; for into this gloomy cavern he was sure the banth had trailed the green man and his captive, and into it he, too, would follow, content to give his life in the service of the woman he loved.

Not an instant did he hesitate, nor yet did he advance rashly; but with ready sword and cautious steps, for the way was dark, he stole on. As he advanced, the obscurity became impenetrable blackness.

CHAPTER V

THE FAIR RACE

Downward along a smooth, broad floor led the strange tunnel, for such Carthoris was now convinced was the nature of the shaft he at first had thought but a cave.

Before him he could hear the occasional low moans of the banth, and presently from behind came a similar uncanny note. Another banth had entered the passageway on *his* trail!

His position was anything but pleasant. His eyes could not penetrate the darkness even to the distinguishing of his hand before his face, while the banths, he knew, could see quite well, though absence of light were utter.

No other sounds came to his ears than the dismal, bloodthirsty moanings of the beast ahead and the beast behind.

The tunnel had led straight, from where he had entered it beneath the side of the rock furthest from the unscaleable cliffs, toward the mighty barrier that had baffled him so long.

Now it was running almost level, and presently he noted a gradual ascent.

The beast behind him was gaining upon him, crowding him perilously close upon the heels of the beast in front. Presently he should have to do battle with one, or both. More firmly he gripped his weapon.

Now he could hear the breathing of the banth at his

heels. Not for much longer could he delay the encounter.

Long since he had become assured that the tunnel led beneath the cliffs to the opposite side of the barrier, and he had hoped that he might reach the moonlit open before being compelled to grapple with either of the monsters.

The sun had been setting as he entered the tunnel, and the way had been sufficiently long to assure him that darkness now reigned upon the world without.

He glanced behind him. Blazing out of the darkness, seemingly not ten paces behind, glared two flaming points of fire. As the savage eyes met his, the beast emitted a frightful roar and then he charged.

To face that savage mountain of onrushing ferocity, to stand unshaken before the hideous fangs that he knew were bared in slavering blood-thirstiness, though he could not see them, required nerves of steel; but of such were the nerves of Carthoris of Helium.

He had the brute's eyes to guide his point, and, as true as the sword hand of his mighty sire, his guided the keen point to one of those blazing orbs, even as he leaped lightly to one side.

With a hideous scream of pain and rage, the wounded banth hurtled, clawing, past him. Then it turned to charge once more; but this time Carthoris saw but a single gleaming point of fiery hate directed upon him.

Again the needle point met its flashing target. Again the horrid cry of the stricken beast reverberated through the rocky tunnel, shocking in its torture-laden shrillness, deafening in its terrific volume.

But now, as it turned to charge again, the man had no guide whereby to direct his point. He heard the scraping of the padded feet upon the rocky floor. He knew the thing was charging down upon him once again, but he could see nothing.

Yet, if he could not see his antagonist, neither could his antagonist now see him.

Leaping, as he thought, to the exact centre of the tunnel, he held his sword point ready on a line with the beast's chest. It was all that he could do, hoping that chance might send the point into the savage heart as he went down beneath the great body.

So quickly was the thing over that Carthoris could scarce believe his senses as the mighty body rushed madly past him. Either he had not placed himself in the centre of the tunnel, or else the blinded banth had erred in its calculations.

However, the huge body missed him by a foot, and the creature continued on down the tunnel as though in pursuit of the prey that had eluded him.

Carthoris, too, followed the same direction, nor was it long before his heart was gladdened by the sight of the moonlit exit from the long, dark passage.

Before him lay a deep hollow, entirely surrounded by gigantic cliffs. The surface of the valley was dotted with enormous trees, a strange sight so far from a Martian waterway. The ground itself was clothed in brilliant scarlet sward, picked out with innumerable patches of gorgeous wild flowers.

Beneath the glorious effulgence of the two moons the scene was one of indescribable loveliness, tinged with the weirdness of strange enchantment.

For only an instant, however, did his gaze rest upon the natural beauties outspread before him. Almost immediately they were riveted upon the figure of a great banth standing across the carcass of a new-killed thoat.

The huge beast, his tawny mane bristling around his hideous head, kept his eyes fixed upon another banth that charged erratically hither and thither, with shrill screams of pain, and horrid roars of hate and rage.

Carthoris quickly guessed that the second brute was the one he had blinded during the fight in the tunnel, but it was the dead thoat that centred his interest more than either of the savage carnivora.

The harness was still upon the body of the huge Martian mount, and Carthoris could not doubt but that this was the very animal upon which the green warrior had borne away Thuvia of Ptarth.

But where were the rider and his prisoner? The Prince

of Helium shuddered as he thought upon the probability of the fate that had overtaken them.

Human flesh is the food most craved by the fierce Barsoomian lion, whose great carcass and giant thews require enormous quantities of meat to sustain them.

Two human bodies would have but whetted the creature's appetite, and that he had killed and eaten the green man and the red girl seemed only too likely to Carthoris. He had left the carcass of the mighty thoat to be devoured after having consumed the more toothsome portion of his banquet.

Now the sightless banth, in its savage, aimless charging and counter-charging, had passed beyond the kill of its fellow, and there the light breeze that was blowing wafted the scent of new blood to its nostrils.

No longer were its movements erratic. With outstretched tail and foaming jaws it charged straight as an arrow, for the body of the thoat and the mighty creature of destruction that stood with forepaws upon the slate-grey side, waiting to defend its meat.

When the charging banth was twenty paces from the dead thoat the killer gave vent to its hideous challenge, and with a mighty spring leaped forward to meet it.

The battle that ensued awed even the warlike Barsoomian. The mad rending, the hideous and deafening roaring, the implacable savagery of the blood-stained beasts held him in the paralysis of fascination, and when it was over and the two creatures, their heads and shoulders torn to ribbons, lay with their dead jaws still buried in each other's bodies, Carthoris tore himself from the spell only by an effort of the will.

Hurrying to the side of the dead thoat, he searched for traces of the girl he feared had shared the thoat's fate, but nowhere could he discover anything to confirm his fears.

With slightly lightened heart he started out to explore the valley, but scarce a dozen steps had he taken when the glistening of a jewelled bauble lying on the sward caught his eye.

As he picked it up his first glance showed him that it was a woman's hair ornament, and emblazoned upon it was the insignia of the royal house of Ptarth.

But, sinister discovery, blood, still wet, splotched the magnificent jewels of the setting.

Carthoris half choked as the dire possibilities which the thing suggested presented themselves to his imagination. Yet he could not, would not believe it.

It was impossible that that radiant creature could have met so hideous an end. It was incredible that the glorious Thuvia should ever cease to be.

Upon his already jewel-encrusted harness, to the strap that crossed his great chest beneath which beat his loyal heart, Carthoris, Prince of Helium, fastened the gleaming thing that Thuvia of Ptarth had worn, and wearing, had made holy to the Heliumite.

Then he proceeded upon his way into the heart of the unknown valley.

For the most part the giant trees shut off his view to any but the most limited distances. Occasionally he caught glimpses of the towering hills that bounded the valley upon every side, and though they stood out clear beneath the light of the two moons, he knew that they were far off, and that the extent of the valley was immense.

For half the night he continued his search, until presently he was brought to a sudden halt by the distant sound of squealing thoats.

Guided by the noise of these habitually angry beasts, he stole forward through the trees until at last he came upon a level, treeless plain, in the centre of which a mighty city reared its burnished domes and vividly coloured towers.

About the walled city the red man saw a huge encampment of the green warriors of the dead sea-bottoms, and as he let his eyes rove carefully over the city he realized that here was no deserted metropolis of a dead past.

But what city could it be? His studies had taught him that in this little-explored portion of Barsoom the fierce tribe of Torquasian green men ruled supreme, and that as yet no red man had succeeded in piercing to the heart of their domain to return again to the world of civilization.

The men of Torquas had perfected huge guns with which their uncanny marksmanship had permitted them to repulse the few determined efforts that near-by red nations had made to explore their country by means of battle fleets of airships.

That he was within the boundary of Torquas, Carthoris was sure, but that there existed there such a wondrous city he never had dreamed, nor had the chronicles of the past even hinted at such a possibility, for the Torquasians were known to live, as did the other green men of Mars, within the deserted cities that dotted the dying planet, nor ever had any green horde built so much as a single edifice, other than the low-walled incubators where their young are hatched by the sun's heat.

The encircling camp of green warriors lay about five hundred yards from the city's walls. Betweeen it and the city was no semblance of breastwork or other protection against rifle or cannon fire; yet distinctly now in the light of the rising sun Carthoris could see many figures moving along the summit of the high wall, and upon the roof tops beyond.

That they were beings like himself he was sure, though they were at too great distance from him for him to be positive that they were red men.

Almost immediately after sunrise the green warriors commenced firing upon the little figures upon the wall. To Carthoris' surprise the fire was not returned, but presently the last of the city's inhabitants had sought shelter from the weird marksmanship of the green men, and no further sign of life was visible beyond the wall.

Then Carthoris, keeping within the shelter of the trees that fringed the plain, began circling the rear of the besiegers' line, hoping against hope that somewhere he would obtain sight of Thuvia of Ptarth, for even now he could not believe that she was dead.

That he was not discovered was a miracle, for mounted warriors were constantly riding back and forth from the camp into the forest; but the long day wore on and still he continued his seemingly fruitless quest, until, near sunset, he came opposite a mighty gate in the city's western wall.

Here seemed to be the principal force of the attacking horde. Here a great platform had been erected whereon Carthoris could see squatting a huge green warrior, surrounded by others of his kind.

This, then, must be the notorious Hortan Gur, Jeddak of Torquas, the fierce old ogre of the south-western hemisphere, as only for a jeddak are platforms raised in temporary camps or upon the march by the green hordes of Barsoom.

As the Heliumite watched he saw another green warrior push his way forward toward the rostrum. Beside him he dragged a captive, and as the surrounding warriors parted to let the two pass, Carthois caught a fleeting glimpse of the prisoner.

His heart leaped in rejoicing. Thuvia of Ptarth still lived!

It was with difficulty that Carthoris restrained the impulse to rush forward to the side of the Ptarthian princess; but in the end his better judgment prevailed, for in the face of such odds he knew that he should have been but throwing away, uselessly, any future opportunity he might have to succour her.

He saw her dragged to the foot of the rostrum. He saw Hortan Gur address her. He could not hear the creature's words, nor Thuvia's reply; but it must have angered the green monster, for Carthoris saw him leap toward the prisoner, striking her a cruel blow across the face with his metal-banded arm.

Then the son of John Carter, Jeddak of Jeddaks, Warlord of Barsoom, went mad. The old, blood-red haze through which his sire had glared at countless foes, floated before his eyes.

His half-Earthly muscles, responding quickly to his will, sent him in enormous leaps and bounds toward the green monster that had struck the woman he loved.

The Torquasians were not looking in the direction of the forest. All eyes had been upon the figures of the girl and their jeddak, and loud was the hideous laughter that rang out in appreciation of the wit of the green emperor's reply to his prisoner's appeal for liberty.

Carthoris had covered about half the distance between the forest and the green warriors, when a new factor succeeded in still further directing the attention of the latter from him.

Upon a high tower within the beleaguered city a man appeared. From his upturned mouth there issued a series of frightful shrieks; uncanny shrieks that swept, shrill and terrifying, across the city's walls, over the heads of the besiegers, and out across the forest to the uttermost confines of the valley.

Once, twice, thrice the fearsome sound smote upon the ears of the listening green men and then far, far off across the broad woods came sharp and clear from the distance an answering shriek.

It was but the first. From every point rose similar savage cries, until the world seemed to tremble to their reverberations.

The green warriors looked nervously this way and that. They knew not fear, as Earth men may know it; but in the face of the unusual their wonted self-assurance deserted them.

And then the great gate in the city wall opposite the platform of Hortan Gur swung suddenly wide. From it issued as strange a sight as Carthoris ever had witnessed, though at the moment he had time to cast but a single fleeting glance at the tall bowmen emerging through the portal behind their long, oval shields; to note their flowing auburn hair; and to realize that the growling things at their side were fierce Barsoomian lions.

Then he was in the midst of the astonished Torquasians. With drawn long-sword he was among them, and to Thuvia of Ptarth, whose startled eyes were the first to fall upon him, it seemed that she was looking upon John Carter himself, so strangely similar to the fighting of the father was that of the son.

Even to the famous fighting smile of the Virginian was the resemblance true. And the sword arm! Ah, the subtleness of it, and the speed!

All about was turmoil and confusion. Green warriors were leaping to the backs of their restive, squealing thoats. Calots were growling out their savage gutturals, whining to be at the throats of the oncoming foemen.

Thar Ban and another by the side of the rostrum had been the first to note the coming of Carthoris, and it was with them he battled for possession of the red girl, while the others hastened to meet the host advancing from the beleaguered city.

Carthoris sought both to defend Thuvia of Ptarth and reach the side of the hideous Hortan Gur that he might avenge the blow the creature had struck the girl.

He succeeded in reaching the rostrum, over the dead bodies of two warriors who had turned to join Thar Ban and his companion in repulsing this adventurous red man, just as Hortan Gur was about to leap from it to the back of his thoat.

The attention of the green warriors turned principally upon the bowmen advancing upon them from the city, and upon the savage banths that paced beside them— cruel beasts of war, infinitely more terrible than their own savage calots.

As Carthoris leaped to the rostrum he drew Thuvia up beside him, and then he turned upon the departing jeddak with an angry challenge and a sword thrust.

As the Heliumite's point pricked his green hide, Hortan Gur turned upon his adversary with a snarl, but at the same instant two of his chieftains called to him to hasten, for the charge of the fair-skinned inhabitants of the city

was developing into a more serious matter than the
Torquasians had anticipated.

Instead of remaining to battle with the red man,
Hortan Gur promised him his attention after he had
disposed of the presumptuous citizens of the walled city,
and, leaping astride his thoat, galloped off to meet the
rapidly advancing bowmen.

The other warriors quickly followed their jeddak, leaving Thuvia and Carthoris alone upon the platform.

Between them and the city raged a terrific battle. The
fair-skinned warriors, armed only with their long bows
and a kind of short-handled war-axe, were almost helpless
beneath the savage mounted green men at close
quarters; but at a distance their sharp arrows did fully as
much execution as the radium projectiles of the green
men.

But if the warriors themselves were outclassed, not so
their savage companions, the fierce banths. Scarce had the
two lines come together when hundreds of these appalling
creatures had leaped among the Torquasians, dragging
warriors from their thoats—dragging down the huge
thoats themselves, and bringing consternation to all
before them.

The numbers of the citizenry, too, was to their advantage, for it seemed that scarce a warrior fell but his
place was taken by a score more, in such a constant
stream did they pour from the city's great gate.

And so it came, what with the ferocity of the banths
and the numbers of the bowmen, that at last the
Torquasians fell back, until presently the platform upon
which stood Carthoris and Thuvia lay directly in the
centre of the fight.

That neither was struck by a bullet or an arrow seemed
a miracle to both; but at last the tide had rolled com-
pletely past them, so that they were alone between the
fighters and the city, except for the dying and the
dead, and a score or so of growling banths, less well
trained than their fellows, who prowled among the corpses
seeking meat.

To Carthoris the strangest part of the battle had been the terrific toll taken by the bowmen with their relatively puny weapons. Nowhere that he could see was there a single wounded green man, but the corpses of their dead lay thick upon the field of battle.

Death seemed to follow instantly the slightest pinprick of a bowman's arrow, nor apparently did one ever miss its goal. There could be but one explanation: the missiles were poison-tipped.

Presently the sounds of conflict died in the distant forest. Quiet reigned, broken only by the growling of the devouring banths. Carthoris turned toward Thuvia of Ptarth. As yet neither had spoken.

"Where are we, Thuvia?" he asked.

The girl looked at him questioningly. His very presence had seemed to proclaim a guilty knowledge of her abduction. How else might he have known the destination of the flier that brought her!

"Who should know better than the Prince of Helium?" she asked in return. "Did he not come hither of his own free will?"

"From Aaanthor I came voluntarily upon the trail of the green man who had stolen you, Thuvia," he replied; "but from the time I left Helium until I awoke above Aaanthor I thought myself bound for Ptarth.

"It had been intimated that I had guilty knowledge of your abduction," he explained simply, "and I was hastening to the jeddak, your father, to convince him of the falsity of the charge, and to give my service to your recovery. Before I left Helium some one tampered with my compass, so that it bore me to Aaanthor instead of to Ptarth. That is all. You believe me?"

"But the warriors who stole me from the garden!" she exclaimed. "After we arrived at Aaanthor they wore the metal of the Prince of Helium. When they took me they were trapped in Dusarian harness. There seemed but a single explanation. Whoever dared the outrage wished to put the onus upon another, should he be detected in the act; but once safely away from Ptarth he felt safe in having his minions return to their own harness."

"You believe that I did this thing, Thuvia?" he asked.

"Ah, Carthoris," she replied sadly, "I did not wish to believe it; but when everything pointed to you—even then I would not believe it."

"I did not do it, Thuvia," he said. "But let me be entirely honest with you. As much as I love your father, as much as I respect Kulan Tith, to whom you are betrothed, as well as I know the frightful consequences that must have followed such an act of mine, hurling into war, as it would, three of the greatest nations of Barsoom—yet, notwithstanding all this, I should not have hesitated to take you thus, Thuvia of Ptarth, had you even hinted that it would not have displeased *you*.

"But you did nothing of the kind, and so I am here, not in my own service, but in yours, and in the service of the man to whom you are promised, to save you for him, if it lies within the power of man to do so," he concluded, almost bitterly.

Thuvia of Ptarth looked into his face for several moments. Her breast was rising and falling as though to some resistless emotion. She half took a step toward him. Her lips parted as though to speak—swiftly and impetuously.

And then she conquered whatever had moved her.

"The future acts of the Prince of Helium," she said coldly, "must constitute the proof of his past honesty of purpose."

Carthoris was hurt by the girl's tone, as much as by the doubt as to his integrity which her words implied.

He had half hoped that she might hint that his love would be acceptable—certainly there was due him at least a little gratitude for his recent acts in her behalf; but the best he received was cold scepticism.

The Prince of Helium shrugged his broad shoulders. The girl noted it, and the little smile that touched his lips, so that it became her turn to be hurt.

Of course she had not meant to hurt him. He might

have known that after what he had said she could not do
anything to encourage him! But he need not have made
his indifference quite so palpable. The men of Helium
were noted for their gallantry—not for boorishness.
Possibly it was the Earth blood that flowed in his veins.

How could she know that the shrug was but Carthoris'
way of attempting, by physical effort, to cast blighting
sorrow from his heart, or that the smile upon his lips
was the fighting smile of his father with which the son
gave outward evidence of the determination he had
reached to submerge his own great love in his efforts to
save Thuvia of Ptarth for another, because he believed
that she loved this other!

He reverted to his original question.

"Where are we?" he asked. "I do not know."

"Nor I," replied the girl. "Those who stole me from
Ptarth spoke among themselves of Aaanthor, so that I
thought it possible that the ancient city to which they
took me was that famous ruin; but where we may be now
I have no idea."

"When the bowmen return we shall doubtless learn all
that there is to know," said Carthoris. "Let us hope that
they prove friendly. What race may they be? Only in the
most ancient of our legends and in the mural paintings of
the deserted cities of the dead sea-bottoms are depicted
such a race of auburn-haired, fair-skinned people. Can it
be that we have stumbled upon a surviving city of the
past which all Barsoom believes buried beneath the
ages?"

Thuvia was looking toward the forest into which the
green men and the pursuing bowmen had disappeared.
From a great distance came the hideous cries of banths,
and an occasional shot.

"It is strange that they do not return," said the girl.

"One would expect to see the wounded limping or being
carried back to the city," replied Carthoris, with a puz-
zled frown. "But how about the wounded nearer the city?
Have they carried them within?"

Both turned their eyes toward the field between them

and the walled city, where the fighting had been most furious.

There were the banths, still growling about their hideous feast.

Carthoris looked at Thuvia in astonishment. Then he pointed toward the field.

"Where are they?" he whispered. *"What has become of their dead and wounded?"*

CHAPTER VI

THE JEDDAK OF LOTHAR

THE GIRL LOOKED her incredulity.

"They lay in piles," she murmured. "There were thousands of them but a minute ago."

"And now," continued Carthoris, "there remain but the banths and the carcasses of the green men."

"They must have sent forth and carried the dead bowmen away while we were talking," said the girl.

"It is impossible!" replied Carthoris. "Thousands of dead lay there upon the field but a moment since. It would have required many hours to have removed them. The thing is uncanny."

"I had hoped," said Thuvia, "that we might find an asylum with these fair-skinned people. Notwithstanding their valour upon the field of battle, they did not strike me as a ferocious or warlike people. I had been about to suggest that we seek entrance to the city, but now I scarce know if I care to venture among people whose dead vanish into thin air."

"Let us chance it," replied Carthoris. "We can be no worse off within their walls than without. Here we may fall prey to the banths or the no less fierce Torquasians. There, at least, we shall find beings moulded after our own images.

"All that causes me to hesitate," he added, "is the danger of taking you past so many banths. A single sword would scarce prevail were even a couple of them to charge simultaneously."

"Do not fear on that score," replied the girl, smiling. "The banths will not harm us."

As she spoke she descended from the platform, and with Carthoris at her side stepped fearlessly out upon the bloody field in the direction of the walled city of mystery.

They had advanced but a short distance when a banth, looking up from its gory feast, descried them. With an angry roar the beast walked quickly in their direction, and at the sound of its voice a score of others followed its example.

Carthoris drew his long-sword. The girl stole a quick glance at his face. She saw the smile upon his lips, and it was as wine to sick nerves; for even upon warlike Barsoom where all men are brave, woman reacts quickly to quiet indifference to danger—to dare-deviltry that is without bombast.

"You may return your sword," she said. "I told you that the banths would not harm us. Look!" and as she spoke she stepped quickly toward the nearest animal.

Carthoris would have leaped after her to protect her, but with a gesture she motioned him back. He heard her calling to the banths in a low, singsong voice that was half purr.

Instantly the great heads went up and all the wicked eyes were riveted upon the figure of the girl. Then, stealthily, they commenced moving toward her. She had stopped now and was standing waiting them.

One, closer to her than the others, hesitated. She spoke to him imperiously, as a master might speak to a refractory hound.

The great carnivore let its head droop, and with tail between its legs came slinking to the girl's feet, and after it came the others until she was entirely surrounded by the savage maneaters.

Turning she led them to where Carthoris stood. They growled a little as they neared the man, but a few sharp words of command put them in their places.

"How do you do it?" exclaimed Carthoris.

"Your father once asked me that same question in the galleries of the Golden Cliffs within the Otz Mountains, beneath the temples of the therns. I could not answer him, nor can I answer you. I do not know whence comes my power over them, but ever since the day that Sator Throg threw me among them in the banth pit of the Holy Therns, and the great creatures fawned upon instead of devouring me, I ever have had the same strange power over them. They come at my call and do my bidding, even as the faithful Woola does the bidding of your mighty sire."

With a word the girl dispersed the fierce pack. Roaring, they returned to their interrupted feast, while Carthoris and Thuvia passed among them toward the walled city.

As they advanced the man looked with wonder upon the dead bodies of those of the green men that had not been devoured or mauled by the banths.

He called the girl's attention to them. No arrows protruded from the great carcasses. Nowhere upon any of them was the sign of mortal wound, nor even slightest scratch or abrasion.

Before the bowmen's dead had disappeared the corpses of the Torquasians had bristled with the deadly arrows of their foes. Where had the slender messengers of death departed? What unseen hand had plucked them from the bodies of the slain?

Despite himself Carthoris could scarce repress a shudder of apprehension as he glanced toward the silent city before them. No longer was sign of life visible upon wall or roof top. All was quiet—brooding, ominous quiet.

Yet he was sure that eyes watched them from somewhere behind that blank wall.

He glanced at Thuvia. She was advancing with wide eyes fixed upon the city gate. He looked in the direction of her gaze, but saw nothing.

His gaze upon her seemed to arouse her as from a lethargy. She glanced up at him, a quick, brave smile

touching her lips, and then, as though the act was in-
voluntary, she came close to his side and placed one of
her hands in his.

He guessed that something within her that was beyond
her conscious control was appealing to him for protection. He threw an arm about her, and thus they crossed
the field. She did not draw away from him. It is doubtful
that she realized that his arm was there, so engrossed
was she in the mystery of the strange city before them.

They stopped before the gate. It was a mighty thing.
From its construction Carthoris could but dimly specu-
late upon its unthinkable antiquity.

It was circular, closing a circular aperture, and the
Heliumite knew from his study of ancient Barsoomian
architecture that it rolled to one side, like a huge wheel,
into an aperture in the wall.

Even such world-old cities as ancient Aaanthor were as
yet undreamed of when the races lived that built such
gates as these.

As he stood speculating upon the identity of this forgotten city, a voice spoke to them from above. Both
looked up. There, leaning over the edge of the high wall,
was a man.

His hair was auburn, his skin fair—fairer even than
that of John Carter, the Virginian. His forehead was high,
his eyes large and intelligent.

The language that he used was intelligible to the two
below, yet there was a marked difference between it and
their Barsoomian tongue.

"Who are you?" he asked. "And what do you here
before the gate of Lothar?"

"We are friends," replied Carthoris. "This be the princess, Thuvia of Ptarth, who was captured by the Torquasian horde. I am Carthoris of Helium, Prince of the
house of Tardos Mors, Jeddak of Helium, and son of John
Carter, Warlord of Mars, and of his wife, Dejah Thoris."

" 'Ptarth'?" repeated the man. " 'Helium'?" He
shook his head. "I never have heard of these places, nor
did I know that there dwelt upon Barsoom a race of thy

strange colour. Where may these cities lie, of which you speak? From our loftiest tower we have never seen another city than Lothar."

Carthoris pointed toward the north-east.

"In that direction lie Helium and Ptarth," he said. "Helium is over eight thousand haads from Lothar, while Ptarth lies nine thousand five hundred haads north-east of Helium." [1]

Still the man shook his head.

"I know of nothing beyond the Lotharian hills," he said. "Naught may live there beside the hideous green hordes of Torquas. They have conquered all Barsoom except this single valley and the city of Lothar. Here we have defied them for countless ages, though periodically they renew their attempts to destroy us. From whence you come I cannot guess unless you be descended from the slaves the Torquasians captured in early times when they reduced the outer world to their vassalage; but we had heard that they destroyed all other races but their own."

Carthoris tried to explain that the Torquasians ruled but a relatively tiny part of the surface of Barsoom, and even this only because their domain held nothing to attract the red race; but the Lotharian could not seem to conceive of anything beyond the valley of Lothar other than a trackless waste peopled by the ferocious green hordes of Torquas.

[1] On Barsoom the *ad* is the basis of linear measurement. It is the equivalent of an Earthly foot, measuring about 11·694 Earth inches. As has been my custom in the past, I have generally translated Barsoomian symbols of time, distance, etc., into their Earthly equivalents, as being more easily understood by Earth readers. For those of a more studious turn of mind it may be interesting to know the Martian table of linear measurement, and so I give it here:

10 sofads = 1 ad.
200 ads = 1 haad.
100 haads = 1 karad.
360 karads = 1 circumference of Mars at equator.

A haad, or Barsoomian mile, contains about 2,339 Earth feet. A karad is one degree. A sofad about 1·17 Earth inches.

After considerable parleying he consented to admit them to the city, and a moment later the wheel-like gate rolled back within its niche, and Thuvia and Carthoris entered the city of Lothar.

All about them were evidences of fabulous wealth. The façades of the buildings fronting upon the avenue within the wall were richly carven, and about the windows and doors were ofttimes set foot-wide borders of precious stones, intricate mosaics, or tablets of beaten gold bearing bas-reliefs depicting what may have been bits of the history of this forgotten people.

He with whom they had conversed across the wall was in the avenue to receive them. About him were a hundred or more men of the same race. All were clothed in flowing robes and all were beardless.

Their attitude was more of fearful suspicion than antagonism. They followed the new-comers with their eyes; but spoke no word to them.

Carthoris could not but notice the fact that though the city had been but a short time before surrounded by a horde of bloodthirsty demons yet none of the citizens appeared to be armed, nor was there sign of soldiery about.

He wondered if all the fighting men had sallied forth in one supreme effort to rout the foe, leaving the city all unguarded. He asked their host.

The man smiled.

"No creature other than a score or so of our sacred banths has left Lothar to-day," he replied.

"But the soldiers—the bowmen!" exclaimed Carthoris. "We saw thousands emerge from this very gate, overwhelming the hordes of Torquas and putting them to rout with their deadly arrows and their fierce banths."

Still the man smiled his knowing smile.

"Look!" he cried, and pointed down a broad avenue before him.

Carthoris and Thuvia followed the direction indicated, and there, marching bravely in the sunlight, they saw advancing toward them a great army of bowmen.

"Ah!" exclaimed Thuvia. "They have returned through

another gate, or perchance these be the troops that remained to defend the city?"

Again the fellow smiled his uncanny smile.

"There are no soldiers in Lothar," he said. "Look!"

Both Carthoris and Thuvia had turned toward him while he spoke, and now as they turned back again toward the advancing regiments their eyes went wide in astonishment, for the broad avenue before them was as deserted as the tomb.

"And those who marched out upon the hordes to-day?" whispered Carthoris. "They, too, were unreal?"

The man nodded.

"But their arrows slew the green warriors," insisted Thuvia.

"Let us go before Tario," replied the Lotharian. "He will tell you that which he deems it best you know. I might tell you too much."

"Who is Tario?" asked Carthoris.

"Jeddak of Lothar," replied the guide, leading them up the broad avenue down which they had but a moment since seen the phantom army marching.

For half an hour they walked along lovely avenues between the most gorgeous buildings that the two had ever seen. Few people were in evidence. Carthoris could not but note the deserted appearance of the mighty city.

At last they came to the royal palace. Carthoris saw it from a distance, and guessing the nature of the magnificent pile wondered that even here there should be so little sign of activity and life.

Not even a single guard was visible before the great entrance gate, nor in the gardens beyond, into which he could see, was there sign of the myriad life that pulses within the precincts of the royal estates of the red jeddaks.

"Here," said their guide, "is the palace of Tario."

As he spoke Carthoris again let his gaze rest upon the wondrous palace. With a startled exclamation he rubbed his eyes and looked again. No! He could not be mistaken. Before the massive gate stood a score of sentries. Within, the avenue leading to the main building was lined on either side by ranks of bowmen. The gardens were dotted with officers and soldiers moving quickly to and fro, as though bent upon the duties of the minute.

What manner of people were these who could conjure an army out of thin air? He glanced toward Thuvia. She, too, evidently had witnessed the transformation.

With a little shudder she pressed more closely toward him.

"What do you make of it?" she whispered. "It is most uncanny."

"I cannot account for it," replied Carthoris, "unless we have gone mad."

Carthoris turned quickly toward the Lotharian. The fellow was smiling broadly.

"I thought that you just said that there were no soldiers in Lothar," said the Heliumite, with a gesture toward the guardsmen. "What are these?"

"Ask Tario," replied the other. "We shall soon be before him."

Nor was it long before they entered a lofty chamber at one end of which a man reclined upon a rich couch that stood upon a high dais.

As the trio approached, the man turned dreamy eyes sleepily upon them. Twenty feet from the dais their conductor halted, and, whispering to Thuvia and Carthoris to follow his example, threw himself headlong to the floor. Then rising to hands and knees, he commenced crawling toward the foot of the throne, swinging his head to and fro and wiggling his body as you have seen a hound do when approaching its master.

Thuvia glanced quickly toward Carthoris. He was standing erect, with high-held head and arms folded across his broad chest. A haughty smile curved his lips.

The man upon the dais was eying him intently, and Carthoris of Helium was looking straight in the other's face.

"Who be these, Jav?" asked the man of him who crawled upon his belly along the floor.

"O Tario, most glorious Jeddak," replied Jav, "these be strangers who came with the hordes of Torquas to our gates, saying that they were prisoners of the green men. They tell strange tales of cities far beyond Lothar."

"Arise, Jav," commanded Tario, "and ask these two why they show not to Tario the respect that is his due."

Jav arose and faced the strangers. At sight of their erect positions his face went livid. He leaped toward them.

"Creatures!" he screamed. "Down! Down upon your bellies before the last of the jeddaks of Barsoom!"

CHAPTER VII

THE PHANTOM BOWMEN

As Jav leaped toward him Carthoris laid his hand upon the hilt of his long-sword. The Lotharian halted. The great apartment was empty save for the four at the dais, yet as Jav stepped back from the menace of the Heliumite's threatening attitude the latter found himself surrounded by a score of bowmen.

From whence had they sprung? Both Carthoris and Thuvia looked their astonishment.

Now the former's sword leaped from its scabbard, and at the same instant the bowmen drew back their slim shafts.

Tario had half raised himself upon one elbow. For the first time he saw the full figure of Thuvia, who had been concealed behind the person of Carthoris.

"Enough!" cried the jeddak, raising a protesting hand, but at that very instant the sword of the Heliumite cut viciously at its nearest antagonist.

As the keen edge reached its goal Carthoris let the point fall to the floor, as with wide eyes he stepped backward in consternation, throwing the back of his left hand across his brow. His steel had cut but empty air—his antagonist had vanished—there were no bowmen in the room!

"It is evident that these are strangers," said Tario to Jav. "Let us first determine that they knowingly affronted us before we take measures for punishment."

Then he turned to Carthoris, but ever his gaze wandered to the perfect lines of Thuvia's glorious figure, which the harness of a Barsoomian princess accentuated rather than concealed.

"Who are you," he asked, "who knows not the etiquette of the court of the last of jeddaks?"

"I am Carthoris, Prince of Helium," replied the Heliumite. "And this is Thuvia, Princess of Ptarth. In the courts of our fathers men do not prostrate themselves before royalty. Not since the First Born tore their immortal goddess limb from limb have men crawled upon their bellies to any throne upon Barsoom. Now think you that the daughter of one mighty jeddak and the son of another would so humiliate themselves?"

Tario looked at Carthoris for a long time. At last he spoke.

"There is no other jeddak upon Barsoom than Tario," he said. "There is no other race than that of Lothar, unless the hordes of Torquas may be dignified by such an appellation. Lotharians are white; your skins are red. There are no women left upon Barsoom. Your companion is a woman."

He half rose from the couch, leaning far forward and pointing an accusing finger at Carthoris.

"You are a lie!" he shrieked. "You are both lies, and you dare to come before Tario, last and mightiest of the jeddaks of Barsoom, and assert your reality. Some one shall pay well for this, Jav, and unless I mistake it is yourself who has dared thus flippantly to trifle with the good nature of your jeddak.

"Remove the man. Leave the woman. We shall see if both be lies. And later, Jav, you shall suffer for your temerity. There be few of us left, but—Komal must be fed. Go!"

Carthoris could see that Jav trembled as he prostrated himself once more before his ruler, and then, rising, turned toward the Prince of Helium.

"Come!" he said.

"And leave the Princess of Ptarth here alone?" cried Carthoris.

Jav brushed closely past him, whispering:

"Follow me—he cannot harm her, except to kill; and that he can do whether you remain or not. We had best go now—trust me."

Carthoris did not understand, but something in the urgency of the other's tone assured him, and so he turned away, but not without a glance toward Thuvia in which he attempted to make her understand that it was in her own interest that he left her.

For answer she turned her back full upon him, but not without first throwing him such a look of contempt that brought the scarlet to his cheek.

Then he hesitated, but Jav seized him by the wrist.

"Come!" he whispered. "Or he will have the bowmen upon you, and this time there will be no escape. Did you not see how futile is your steel against thin air!"

Carthoris turned unwillingly to follow. As the two left the room he turned to his companion.

"If I may not kill thin air," he asked, "how, then, shall I fear that thin air may kill me?"

"You saw the Torquasians fall before the bowmen?" asked Jav.

Carthoris nodded.

"So would you fall before them, and without one single chance for self-defence or revenge."

As they talked Jav led Carthoris to a small room in one of the numerous towers of the palace. Here were couches, and Jav bid the Heliumite be seated.

For several minutes the Lotharian eyed his prisoner, for such Carthoris now realized himself to be.

"I am half convinced that you are real," he said at last.

Carthoris laughed.

"Of course I am real," he said. "What caused you to doubt it? Can you not see me, feel me?"

"So may I see and feel the bowmen," replied Jav, "and yet we all know that they, at least, are not real."

Carthoris showed by the expression of his face his

puzzlement at each new reference to the mysterious bow-men—the vanishing soldiery of Lothar.

"What, then, may they be?" he asked.

"You really do not know?" asked Jav.

Carthoris shook his head negatively.

"I can almost believe that you have told us the truth and that you are really from another part of Barsoom, or from another world. But tell me, in your own country have you no bowmen to strike terror to the hearts of the green hordesmen as they slay in company with the fierce banths of war?"

"We have soldiers," replied Carthoris. "We of the red race are all soldiers, but we have no bowmen to defend us, such as yours. We defend ourselves."

"You go out and get killed by your enemies!" cried Jav incredulously.

"Certainly," replied Carthoris. "How do the Lotharians?"

"You have seen," replied the other. "We send out our deathless archers—deathless because they are lifeless, existing only in the imaginations of our enemies. It is really our giant minds that defend us, sending out legions of imaginary warriors to materialize before the mind's eye of the foe.

"They see them—they see their bows drawn back—they see their slender arrows speed with unerring precision toward their hearts. And they die—killed by the power of suggestion."

"But the archers that are slain?" exclaimed Carthoris. "You call them deathless, and yet I saw their dead bodies piled high upon the battlefield. How may that be?"

"It is but to lend reality to the scene," replied Jav. "We picture many of our own defenders killed that the Torquasians may not guess that there are really no flesh and blood creatures opposing them.

"Once that truth became implanted in their minds, it is the theory of many of us, no longer would they fall prey to the suggestion of the deadly arrows, for greater would be the suggestion of the truth, and the more powerful suggestion would prevail—it is law."

"And the banths?" questioned Carthoris. "They, too, were but creatures of suggestion?"

"Some of them were real," replied Jav. "Those that accompanied the archers in pursuit of the Torquasians were unreal. Like the archers, they never returned, but, having served their purpose, vanished with the bowmen when the rout of the enemy was assured.

"Those that remained about the field were real. Those we loosed as scavengers to devour the bodies of the dead of Torquas. This thing is demanded by the realists among us. I am a realist. Tario is an etherealist.

"The etherealists maintain that there is no such thing as matter—that all is mind. They say that none of us exists, except in the imagination of his fellows, other than as an intangible, invisible mentality.

"According to Tario, it is but necessary that we all unite in imagining that there are no dead Torquasians beneath our walls, and there will be none, nor any need of scavenging banths."

"You, then, do not hold Tario's beliefs?" asked Carthoris.

"In part only," replied the Lotharian. "I believe, in fact I know, that there are some truly ethereal creatures. Tario is one, I am convinced. He has no existence except in the imaginations of his people.

"Of course, it is the contention of all us realists that all etherealists are but figments of the imagination. They contend that no food is necessary, nor do they eat; but any one of the most rudimentary intelligence must realize that food is a necessity to creatures having actual existence."

"Yes," agreed Carthoris, "not having eaten to-day I can readily agree with you."

"Ah, pardon me," exclaimed Jav. "Pray be seated and satisfy your hunger," and with a wave of his hand he indicated a bountifully laden table that had not been there an instant before he spoke. Of that Carthoris was positive, for he had searched the room diligently with his eyes several times.

"It is well," continued Jav, "that you did not fall into the hands of an etherealist. Then, indeed, would you have gone hungry."

"But," exclaimed Carthoris, "this is not real food—it was not here an instant since, and real food does not materialize out of thin air."

Jav looked hurt.

"There is no real food or water in Lothar," he said; "nor has there been for countless ages. Upon such as you now see before you have we existed since the dawn of history. Upon such, then, may you exist."

"But I thought you were a realist," exclaimed Carthoris.

"Indeed," cried Jav, "what more realistic than this bounteous feast? It is just here that we differ most from the etherealists. They claim that it is unnecessary to imagine food; but we have found that for the maintenance of life we must thrice daily sit down to hearty meals.

"The food that one eats is supposed to undergo certain chemical changes during the process of digestion and assimilation, the result, of course, being the rebuilding of wasted tissue.

"Now we all know that mind is all, though we may differ in the interpretation of its various manifestations. Tario maintains that there is no such thing as substance, all being created from the substanceless matter of the brain.

"We realists, however, know better. We know that mind has the power to maintain substance even though it may not be able to create substance—the latter is still an open question. And so we know that in order to maintain our physical bodies we must cause all our organs properly to function.

"This we accomplish by materializing food-thoughts, and by partaking of the food thus created. We chew, we swallow, we digest. All our organs function precisely as if we had partaken of material food. And what is the result? What must be the result? The chemical changes take place through both direct and indirect suggestion, and we live and thrive."

Carthoris eyed the food before him. It seemed real enough. He lifted a morsel to his lips. There was substance indeed. And flavour as well. Yes, even his palate was deceived.

Jav watched him, smiling, as he ate.

"Is it not entirely satisfying?" he asked.

"I must admit that it is," replied Carthoris. "But tell me, how does Tario live, and the other etherealists who maintain that food is unnecessary?"

Jav scratched his head.

"That is a question we often discuss," he replied. "It is the strongest evidence we have of the non-existence of the etherealists; but who may know other than Komal?"

"Who is Komal?" asked Carthoris. "I heard your jeddak speak of him."

Jav bent low toward the ear of the Heliumite, looking fearfully about before he spoke.

"Komal is the essence," he whispered. "Even the etherealists admit that mind itself must have substance in order to transmit to imaginings the appearance of substance. For if there really was no such thing as substance it could not be suggested—what never has been cannot be imagined. Do you follow me?"

"I am groping," replied Carthoris dryly.

"So the essence must be substance," continued Jav. "Komal is the essence of the All, as it were. He is maintained by substance. He eats. He eats the real. To be explicit, he eats the realists. That is Tario's work.

"He says that inasmuch as we maintain that we alone are real we should, to be consistent, admit that we alone are proper food for Komal. Sometimes, as to-day, we find other food for him. He is very fond of Torquasians."

"And Komal is a man?" asked Carthoris.

"He is All, I told you," replied Jav. "I know not how to explain him in words that you will understand. He is the beginning and the end. All life emanates from Komal, since the substance which feeds the brain with imaginings radiates from the body of Komal.

"Should Komal cease to eat, all life upon Barsoom would cease to be. He cannot die, but he might cease to eat, and, thus, to radiate."

"And he feeds upon the men and women of your belief?" cried Carthoris.

"Women!" exclaimed Jav. "There are no women in Lothar. The last of the Lotharian females perished ages since, upon that cruel and terrible journey across the muddy plains that fringed the half-dried seas, when the green hordes scourged us across the world to this our last hiding-place—our impregnable fortress of Lothar.

"Scarce twenty thousand men of all the countless millions of our race lived to reach Lothar. Among us were no women and no children. All these had perished by the way.

"As time went on, we, too, were dying and the race fast approaching extinction, when the Great Truth was revealed to us, that mind is all. Many more died before we perfected our powers, but at last we were able to defy death when we fully understood that death was merely a state of mind.

"Then came the creation of mind-people, or rather the materialization of imaginings. We first put these to practical use when the Torquasians discovered our retreat, and fortunate for us it was that it required ages of search upon their part before they found the single tiny entrance to the valley of Lothar.

"That day we threw our first bowmen against them. The intention was purely to frighten them away by the vast numbers of bowmen which we could muster upon our walls. All Lothar bristled with the bows and arrows of our ethereal host.

"But the Torquasians did not frighten. They are lower than the beasts—they know no fear. They rushed upon our walls, and standing one upon the shoulders of others they built human approaches to the wall tops, and were on the very point of surging in upon us and overwhelming us.

"Not an arrow had been discharged by our bowmen—we did but cause them to run to and fro along the wall top, screaming taunts and threats at the enemy.

"Presently I thought to attempt the thing—*the great thing*. I centred all my mighty intellect upon the bowmen of my own creation—each of us produces and directs as many bowmen as his mentality and imagination is capable of.

"I caused them to fit arrows to their bows for the first time. I made them take aim at the hearts of the green men. I made the green men see all this, and then I made them see the arrows fly, and I made them think that the points pierced their hearts.

"It was all that was necessary. By hundreds they toppled from our walls, and when my fellows saw what I had done they were quick to follow my example, so that presently the hordes of Torquas had retreated beyond the range of our arrows.

"We might have killed them at any distance, but one rule of war we have maintained from the first—the rule of realism. We do nothing, or rather we cause our bowmen to do nothing within sight of the enemy that is beyond the understanding of the foe. Otherwise they might guess the truth, and that would be the end of us.

"But after the Torquasians had retreated beyond bowshot, they turned upon us with their terrible rifles, and by constant popping at us made life miserable within our walls.

"So then I bethought the scheme to hurl our bowmen through the gates upon them. You have seen this day how well it works. For ages they have come down upon us at intervals, but always with the same results."

"And all this is due to your intellect, Jav?" asked Carthoris. "I should think that you would be high in the councils of your people."

"I am," replied Jav, proudly. "I am next to Tario."

"But why, then, your cringing manner of approaching the throne?"

"Tario demands it. He is jealous of me. He only awaits the slightest excuse to feed me to Komal. He fears that I may some day usurp his power."

Carthoris suddenly sprang from the table.

"Jav!" he exclaimed. "I am a beast! Here I have been eating my fill, while the Princess of Ptarth may perchance be still without food. Let us return and find some means of furnishing her with nourishment."

The Lotharian shook his head.

"Tario would not permit it," he said. "He will, doubtless, make an etherealist of her."

"But I must go to her," insisted Carthoris. "You say that there are no women in Lothar. Then she must be among men, and if this be so I intend to be near where I may defend her if the need arises."

"Tario will have his way," insisted Jav. "He sent you away and you may not return until he sends for you."

"Then I shall go without waiting to be sent for."

"Do not forget the bowmen," cautioned Jav.

"I do not forget them," replied Carthoris, but he did not tell Jav that he remembered something else that the Lotharian had let drop—something that was but a conjecture, possibly, and yet one well worth pinning a forlorn hope to, should necessity arise.

Carthoris started to leave the room. Jav stepped before him, barring his way.

"I have learned to like you, red man," he said; "but do not forget that Tario is still my jeddak, and that Tario has commanded that you remain here."

Carthoris was about to reply, when there came faintly to the ears of both a woman's cry for help.

With a sweep of his arm the Prince of Helium brushed the Lotharian aside, and with drawn sword sprang into the corridor without.

CHAPTER VIII

THE HALL OF DOOM

As THUVIA of Ptarth saw Carthoris depart from the presence of Tario, leaving her alone with the man, a sudden qualm of terror seized her.

There was an air of mystery pervading the stately chamber. Its furnishings and appointments bespoke wealth and culture, and carried the suggestion that the room was often the scene of royal functions which filled it to its capacity.

And yet nowhere about her, in antechamber or corridor, was there sign of any other being than herself and the recumbent figure of Tario, the jeddak, who watched her through half-closed eyes from the gorgeous trappings of his regal couch.

For a time after the departure of Jav and Carthoris the man eyed her intently. Then he spoke.

"Come nearer," he said, and, as she approached: "Whose creature are you? Who has dared materialize his imaginings of woman? It is contrary to the customs and the royal edicts of Lothar. Tell me, woman, from whose brain have you sprung? Jav's? No, do not deny it. I know that it could be no other than that envious realist. He seeks to tempt me. He would see me fall beneath the spell of your charms, and then he, your master, would direct my destiny and—my end. I see it all! I see it all!"

The blood of indignation and anger had been rising to Thuvia's face. Her chin was up, a haughty curve upon her perfect lips.

"I know naught," she cried, "of what you are prating! I am Thuvia, Princess of Ptarth. I am no man's 'creature.' Never before to-day did I lay eyes upon him you call Jav, nor upon your ridiculous city, of which even the greatest nations of Barsoom have never dreamed.

"My charms are not for you, nor such as you. They are not for sale or barter, even though the price were a real throne. And as for using them to win your worse than futile power——" She ended her sentence with a shrug of her shapely shoulders, and a little scornful laugh.

When she had finished Tario was sitting upon the edge of his couch, his feet upon the floor. He was leaning forward with eyes no longer half closed, but wide with a startled expression in them.

He did not seem to note the *lèse majesté* of her words and manner. There was evidently something more startling and compelling about her speech than that.

Slowly he came to his feet.

"By the fangs of Komal!" he muttered. "But you are *real*! A *real* woman! No dream! No vain and foolish figment of the mind!"

He took a step toward her, with hands outstretched.

"Come!" he whispered. "Come, woman! For countless ages have I dreamed that some day you would come. And now that you are here I can scarce believe the testimony of my eyes. Even now, knowing that you are real, I still half dread that you may be a lie."

Thuvia shrank back. She thought the man mad. Her hand stole to the jewelled hilt of her dagger. The man saw the move, and stopped. A cunning expression entered his eyes. Then they became at once dreamy and penetrating as they fairly bored into the girl's brain.

Thuvia suddenly felt a change coming over her. What the cause of it she did not guess; but somehow the man before her began to assume a new relationship within her heart.

No longer was he a strange and mysterious enemy, but an old and trusted friend. Her hand slipped from the dagger's hilt. Tario came closer. He spoke gentle, friendly words, and she answered him in a voice that seemed hers and yet another's.

He was beside her now. His hand was up her shoulder. His eyes were down-bent toward hers. She looked up into his face. His gaze seemed to bore straight through her to some hidden spring of sentiment within her.

Her lips parted in sudden awe and wonder at the strange revealment of her inner self that was being laid bare before her consciousness. She had known Tario for ever. He was more than friend to her. She moved a little closer to him. In one swift flood of light she knew the truth. She loved Tario, Jeddak of Lothar! She had always loved him.

The man, seeing the success of his strategy, could not restrain a faint smile of satisfaction. Whether there was something in the expression of his face, or whether from Carthoris of Helium in a far chamber of the palace came a more powerful suggestion, who may say? But something there was that suddenly dispelled the strange, hypnotic influence of the man.

As though a mask had been torn from her eyes, Thuvia suddenly saw Tario as she had formerly seen him, and, accustomed as she was to the strange manifestations of highly developed mentality which are common upon Barsoom, she quickly guessed enough of the truth to know that she was in grave danger.

Quickly she took a step backward, tearing herself from his grasp. But the momentary contact had aroused within Tario all the long-buried passions of his loveless existence.

With a muffled cry he sprang upon her, throwing his arms about her and attempting to drag her lips to his.

"Woman!" he cried. "Lovely woman! Tario would make you queen of Lothar. Listen to me! Listen to the love of the last of the jeddaks of Barsoom."

Thuvia struggled to free herself from his embrace.

"Stop, creature!" she cried. "Stop! I do not love you. Stop, or I shall scream for help!"

Tario laughed in her face.

" 'Scream for help,' " he mimicked. "And who within the halls of Lothar is there who might come in answer to your call? Who would dare enter the presence of Tario, unsummoned?"

"There is one," she replied, "who would come, and, coming, dare to cut you down upon your own throne, if he thought that you had offered affront to Thuvia of Ptarth!"

"Who, Jav?" asked Tario.

"Not Jav, nor any other soft-skinned Lotharian," she replied; "but a real man, a real warrior—Carthoris of Helium!"

Again the man laughed at her.

"You forget the bowmen," he reminded her. "What could your red warrior accomplish against my fearless legions?"

Again he caught her roughly to him, dragging her towards his couch.

"If you will not be my queen," he said, "you shall be my slave."

"Neither!" cried the girl.

As she spoke the single word there was a quick move of her right hand; Tario, releasing her, staggered back, both hands pressed to his side. At the same instant the room filled with bowmen, and then the jeddak of Lothar sank senseless to the marble floor.

At the instant that he lost consciousness the bowmen were about to release their arrows into Thuvia's heart. Involuntarily she gave a single cry for help, though she knew that not even Carthoris of Helium could save her now.

Then she closed her eyes and waited for the end. No slender shafts pierced her tender side. She raised her lids to see what stayed the hand of her executioners.

The room was empty save for herself and the still

form of the jeddak of Lothar lying at her feet, a little
pool of crimson staining the white marble of the floor
beside him. Tario was unconscious.

Thuvia was amazed. Where were the bowmen? Why
had they not loosed their shafts? What could it all mean?

An instant before the room had been mysteriously filled
with armed men, evidently called to protect their jeddak; yet now, with the evidence of her deed plain before
them, they had vanished as mysteriously as they had
come, leaving her alone with the body of their ruler,
into whose side she had slipped her long, keen blade.

The girl glanced apprehensively about, first for signs
of the return of the bowmen, and then for some means of
escape.

The wall behind the dais was pierced by two small
doorways, hidden by heavy hangings. Thuvia was running quickly towards one of these when she heard the
clank of a warrior's metal at the end of the apartment behind her.

Ah, if she had put an instant more of time she could
have reached that screening arras and, perchance, have
found some avenue of escape behind it; but now it was
too late—she had been discovered!

With a feeling that was akin to apathy she turned to
meet her fate, and there, before her, running swiftly
across the broad chamber to her side, was Carthoris, his
naked long-sword gleaming in his hand.

For days she had doubted the intentions of the
Heliumite. She had thought him a party to her abduction.
Since Fate had thrown them together she had scarce
favoured him with more than the most perfunctory replies
to his remarks, unless at such times as the weird and
uncanny happenings at Lothar had surprised her out of
her reserve.

She knew that Carthoris of Helium would fight for her;
but whether to save her for himself or another, she was
in doubt.

He knew that she was promised to Kulan Tith, Jeddak
of Kaol, but if he had been instrumental in her abduction,

his motives could not be prompted by loyalty to his friend, or regard for her honour.

And yet, as she saw him coming across the marble floor of the audience chamber of Tario of Lothar, his fine eyes filled with apprehension for her safety, his splendid figure personifying all that is finest in the fighting men of martial Mars, she could not believe that any faintest trace of perfidy lurked beneath so glorious an exterior.

Never, she thought, in all her life had the sight of any man been so welcome to her. It was with difficulty that she refrained from rushing forward to meet him.

She knew that he loved her; but, in time, she recalled that she was promised to Kulan Tith. Not even might she trust herself to show too great gratitude to the Heliumite, lest he misunderstand.

Carthoris was by her side now. His quick glance had taken in the scene within the room—the still figure of the jeddak sprawled upon the floor—the girl hastening toward a shrouded exit.

"Did he harm you, Thuvia?" he asked.

She held up her crimsoned blade that he might see it. "No," she said, "he did not harm me."

A grim smile lighted Carthoris' face.

"Praised be our first ancestor!" he murmured. "And now let us see if we may not make good our escape from this accursed city before the Lotharians discover that their jeddak is no more."

With the firm authority that sat so well upon him in whose veins flowed the blood of John Carter of Virginia and Dejah Thoris of Helium, he grasped her hand and, turning back across the hall, strode toward the great doorway through which Jav had brought them into the presence of the jeddak earlier in the day.

They had almost reached the threshold when a figure sprang into the apartment through another entrance. It was Jav. He, too, took in the scene within at a glance.

Carthoris turned to face him, his sword ready in

his hand, and his great body shielding the slender figure of the girl.

"Come, Jav of Lothar!" he cried. "Let us face the issue at once, for only one of us may leave this chamber alive with Thuvia of Ptarth," Then, seeing that the man wore no sword, he exclaimed: "Bring on your bowmen, then, or come with us as my prisoner until we have safely passed the outer portals of thy ghostly city."

"You have killed Tario!" exclaimed Jav, ignoring the other's challenge. "You have killed Tario! I see his blood upon the floor—real blood—real death. Tario was, after all, as real as I. Yet he was an etherealist. He would not materialize his sustenance. Can it be that they are right? Well, we, too, are right. And all these ages we have been quarrelling—each saying that the other was wrong!

"However, he is dead now. Of that I am glad. Now shall Jav come into his own. Now shall Jav be Jeddak of Lothar!"

As he finished, Tario opened his eyes and then quickly sat up.

"Traitor! Assassin!" he screamed, and then: "Kadar! Kadar!" which is the Barsoomian for guard.

Jav went sickly white. He fell upon his belly, wriggling toward Tario.

"Oh, my Jeddak, my Jeddak!" he whimpered. "Jav had no hand in this. Jav, your faithful Jav, but just this instant entered the apartment to find you lying prone upon the floor and these two strangers about to leave. How it happened I know not. Believe me, most glorious Jeddak!"

"Cease, knave!" cried Tario. "I heard your words: 'However, he is dead now. Of that I am glad. Now shall Jav come into his own. Now shall Jav be Jeddak of Lothar."

"At last, traitor, I have found you out. Your own words have condemned you as surely as the acts of these red creatures have sealed their fates—unless——" He paused. "Unless the woman——"

But he got no further. Carthoris guessed what he would have said, and before the words could be uttered he had sprung forward and struck the man across the mouth with his open palm.

Tario frothed in rage and mortification.

"And should you again affront the Princess of Ptarth," warned the Heliumite, "I shall forget that you wear no sword—not for ever may I control my itching sword hand."

Tario shrank back toward the little doorways behind the dais. He was trying to speak, but so hideously were the muscles of his face working that he could utter no word for several minutes. At last he managed to articulate intelligibly.

"Die!" he shrieked. "Die!" and then he turned toward the exit at his back.

Jav leaped forward, screaming in terror.

"Have pity, Tario! Have pity! Remember the long ages that I have served you faithfully. Remember all that I have done for Lothar. Do not condemn me now to the death hideous. Save me! Save me!"

But Tario only laughed a mocking laugh and continued to back toward the hangings that hid the little doorway.

Jav turned toward Carthoris.

"Stop him!" he screamed. "Stop him! If you love life, let him not leave this room," and as he spoke he leaped in pursuit of his jeddak.

Carthoris followed Jav's example, but the "last of the jeddaks of Barsoom" was too quick for them. By the time they reached the arras behind which he had disappeared, they found a heavy stone door blocking their further progress.

Jav sank to the floor in a spasm of terror.

"Come, man!" cried Carthoris. "We are not dead yet. Let us hasten to the avenues and make an attempt to leave the city. We are still alive, and while we live we may yet endeavour to direct our own destinies. Of what avail, to sink spineless to the floor? Come, be a man!"

Jav but shook his head.

"Did you not hear him call the guards?" he moaned. "Ah, if we could have but intercepted him! Then there might have been hope; but, alas, he was too quick for us."

"Well, well," exclaimed Carthoris impatiently. "What if he did call the guards? There will be time enough to worry about that after they come—at present I see no indication that they have any idea of over-exerting themselves to obey their jeddak's summons."

Jav shook his head mournfully.

"You do not understand," he said. "The guards have already come—and gone. They have done their work and we are lost. Look to the various exits."

Carthoris and Thuvia turned their eyes in the direction of the several doorways which pierced the walls of the great chamber. Each was tightly closed by huge stone doors.

"Well?" asked Carthoris.

"We are to die the death," whispered Jav faintly.

Further than that he would not say. He just sat upon the edge of the jeddak's couch and waited.

Carthoris moved to Thuvia's side, and, standing there with naked sword, he let his brave eyes roam ceaselessly about the great chamber, that no foe might spring upon them unseen.

For what seemed hours no sound broke the silence of their living tomb. No sign gave their executioners of the time or manner of their death. The suspense was terrible. Even Carthoris of Helium began to feel the terrible strain upon his nerves. If he could but know how and whence the hand of death was to strike, he could meet it unafraid, but to suffer longer the hideous tension of this blighting ignorance of the plans of their assassins was telling upon him grievously.

Thuvia of Ptarth drew quite close to him. She felt safer with the feel of his arm against hers, and with the contact of her the man took a new grip upon himself. With his old-time smile he turned toward her.

"It would seem that they are trying to frighten us to death," he said, laughing; "and, shame be upon me that I should confess it, I think they were close to accomplishing their designs upon me."

She was about to make some reply when a fearful shriek broke from the lips of the Lotharian.

"The end is coming!" he cried. "The end is coming! The floor! The floor! Oh, Komal, be merciful!"

Thuvia and Carthoris did not need to look at the floor to be aware of the strange movement that was taking place.

Slowly the marble flagging was sinking in all directions toward the centre. At first the movement, being gradual, was scarce noticeable; but presently the angle of the floor became such that one might stand easily only by bending one knee considerably.

Jav was shrieking still, and clawing at the royal couch that had already commenced to slide toward the centre of the room, where both Thuvia and Carthoris suddenly noted a small orifice which grew in diameter as the floor assumed more closely a funnel-like contour.

Now it became more and more difficult to cling to the dizzy inclination of the smooth and polished marble. Carthoris tried to support Thuvia, but himself commenced to slide and slip toward the ever-enlarging aperture.

Better to cling to the smooth stone he kicked off his sandals of zitidar hide and with his bare feet braced himself against the sickening tilt, at the same time throwing his arms supportingly about the girl.

In her terror her own hands clasped about the man's neck. Her cheek was close to his. Death, unseen and of unknown form, seemed close upon them, and because unseen and unknowable infinitely more terrifying.

"Courage, my princess," he whispered.

She looked up into his face to see smiling lips above hers and brave eyes, untouched by terror, drinking deeply of her own.

Then the floor sagged and tilted more swiftly. There was a sudden slipping rush as they were precipitated toward the aperture.

Jav's screams rose weird and horrible in their ears, and then the three found themselves piled upon the royal couch of Tario, which had stuck within the aperture at the base of the marble funnel.

For a moment they breathed more freely, but presently they discovered that the aperture was continuing to enlarge. The couch slipped downward. Jav shrieked again. There was a sickening sensation as they felt all let go beneath them, as they fell through darkness to an unknown death.

CHAPTER IX

THE BATTLE IN THE PLAIN

THE DISTANCE from the bottom of the funnel to the floor of the chamber beneath it could not have been great, for all three of the victims of Tario's wrath alighted unscathed.

Carthoris, still clasping Thuvia tightly to his breast, came to the ground catlike, upon his feet, breaking the shock for the girl. Scarce had his feet touched the rough stone flagging of this new chamber than his sword flashed out ready for instant use. But though the room was lighted, there was no sign of enemy about.

Carthoris looked toward Jav. The man was pasty white with fear.

"What is to be our fate?" asked the Heliumite. "Tell me, man! Shake off your terror long enough to tell me, so I may be prepared to sell my life and that of the Princess of Ptarth as dearly as possible."

"Komal!" whispered Jav. "We are to be devoured by Komal!"

"Your deity?" asked Carthoris.

The Lotharian nodded his head. Then he pointed toward a low doorway at one end of the chamber.

"From thence will he come upon us. Lay aside your puny sword, fool. It will but enrage him the more and make our sufferings the worse."

Carthoris smiled, gripping his long-sword the more firmly.

Presently Jav gave a horrified moan, at the same time pointing toward the door.

"He has come," he whimpered.

Carthoris and Thuvia looked in the direction the Lotharian had indicated, expecting to see some strange and fearful creature in human form; but to their astonishment they saw the broad head and great-maned shoulders of a huge banth, the largest that either ever had seen.

Slowly and with dignity the mighty beast advanced into the room. Jav had fallen to the floor, and was wriggling his body in the same servile manner that he had adopted toward Tario. He spoke to the fierce beast as he would have spoken to a human being, pleading with it for mercy.

Carthoris stepped between Thuvia and the banth, his sword ready to contest the beast's victory over them. Thuvia turned toward Jav.

"Is this Komal, your god?" she asked.

Jav nodded affirmatively. The girl smiled, and then, brushing past Carthoris, she stepped swiftly toward the growling carnivore.

In low, firm tones she spoke to it as she had spoken to the banths of the Golden Cliffs and the scavengers before the walls of Lothar.

The beast ceased its growling. With lowered head and catlike purr, it came slinking to the girl's feet. Thuvia turned toward Carthoris.

"It is but a banth," she said. "We have nothing to fear from it."

Carthoris smiled.

"I did not fear it," he replied, "for I, too, believed it to be only a banth, and I have my long-sword."

Jav sat up and gazed at the spectacle before him— the slender girl weaving her fingers in the tawny mane of the huge creature that he had thought divine, while Komal rubbed his hideous snout against her side.

"So this is your god!" laughed Thuvia.

Jav looked bewildered. He scarce knew whether he

dare chance offending Komal or not, for so strong is
the power of superstition that even though we know
that we have been reverencing a sham, yet still we
hesitate to admit the validity of our new-found convic-
tions.

"Yes," he said, "this is Komal. For ages the enemies
of Tario have been hurled to this pit to fill his maw,
for Komal must be fed."

"Is there any way out of this chamber to the avenues
of the city?" asked Carthoris.

Jav shrugged.

"I do not know," he replied. "Never have I been
here before, nor ever have I cared to do so."

"Come," suggested Thuvia, "let us explore. There
must be a way out."

Together the three approached the doorway through
which Komal had entered the apartment that was to
have witnessed their deaths. Beyond was a low-roofed
lair, with a small door at the far end.

This, to their delight, opened to the lifting of an ordinary latch, letting them into a circular arena, surrounded by tiers of seats.

"Here is where Komal is fed in public," explained
Jav. "Had Tario dared it would have been here that
our fates had been sealed; but he feared too much thy
keen blade, red man, and so he hurled us all downward
to the pit. I did not know how closely connected were
the two chambers. Now we may easily reach the avenues
and the city gates. Only the bowmen may dispute the
right of way, and, knowing their secret, I doubt that
they have power to harm us."

Another door led to a flight of steps that rose from
the arena level upward through the seats to an exit at
the back of the hall. Beyond this was a straight, broad
corridor, running directly through the palace to the
gardens at the side.

No one appeared to question them as they advanced,
mighty Komal pacing by the girl's side.

"Where are the people of the palace—the jeddak's retinue?" asked Carthoris. "Even in the city streets as we came through I scarce saw sign of a human being, yet all about are evidences of a mighty population."

Jav sighed.

"Poor Lothar," he said. "It is indeed a city of ghosts. There are scarce a thousand of us left, who once were numbered in the millions. Our great city is peopled by the creatures of our own imaginings. For our own needs we do not take the trouble to materialize these peoples of our brain, yet they are apparent to us.

"Even now I see great throngs lining the avenue, hastening to and fro in the round of their duties. I see women and children laughing on the balconies—these we are forbidden to materialize; but yet I see them—they are here. . . . But why not?" he mused. "No longer need I fear Tario—he has done his worst, and failed. Why not indeed?

"Stay, friends," he continued. "Would you see Lothar in all her glory?"

Carthoris and Thuvia nodded their assent, more out of courtesy than because they fully grasped the import of his mutterings.

Jav gazed at them penetratingly for an instant, then, with a wave of his hand, cried: "Look!"

The sight that met them was awe-inspiring. Where before there had been naught but deserted pavements and scarlet swards, yawning windows and tenantless doors, now swarmed a countless multitude of happy, laughing people.

"It is the past," said Jav in a low voice. "They do not see us—they but live the old dead past of ancient Lothar—the dead and crumbled Lothar of antiquity, which stood upon the shore of Throxus, mightiest of the five oceans.

"See those fine, upstanding men swinging along the broad avenue? See the young girls and the women smile upon them? See the men greet them with love and respect? Those be seafarers coming up from their ships which lie at the quays at the city's edge.

"Brave men, they—ah, but the glory of Lothar has faded! See their weapons. They alone bore arms, for they crossed the five seas to strange places where dangers were. With their passing passed the martial spirit of the Lotharians, leaving, as the ages rolled by, a race of spineless cowards.

"We hated war, and so we trained not our youth in warlike ways. Thus followed our undoing, for when the seas dried and the green hordes encroached upon us we could do naught but flee. But we remembered the seafaring bowmen of the days of our glory—it is the memory of these which we hurl upon our enemies."

As Jav ceased speaking, the picture faded, and once more the three took up their way toward the distant gates, along deserted avenues.

Twice they sighted Lotharians of flesh and blood. At sight of them and the huge banth which they must have recognized as Komal, the citizens turned and fled.

"They will carry word of our flight to Tario," cried Jav, "and soon he will send his bowmen after us. Let us hope that our theory is correct, and that their shafts are powerless against minds cognizant of their unreality. Otherwise we are doomed.

"Explain, red man, to the woman the truths that I have explained to you, that she may meet the arrows with a stronger counter-suggestion of immunity."

Carthoris did as Jav bid him; but they came to the great gates without sign of pursuit developing. Here Jav set in motion the mechanism that rolled the huge, wheellike gate aside, and a moment later the three, accompanied by the banth, stepped out into the plain before Lothar.

Scarce had they covered a hundred yards when the sound of many men shouting arose behind them. As they turned they saw a company of bowmen debouching upon the plain from the gate through which they had but just passed.

Upon the wall above the gate were a number of Lotharians, among whom Jav recognized Tario. The jeddak stood glaring at them, evidently concentrating all the forces of his trained mind upon them. That he was making a supreme effort to render his imaginary creatures deadly was apparent.

Jav turned white, and commenced to tremble. At the crucial moment he appeared to lose the courage of his conviction. The great banth turned back toward the advancing bowmen and growled. Carthoris placed himself between Thuvia and the enemy and, facing them, awaited the outcome of their charge.

Suddenly an inspiration came to Carthoris.

"Hurl your own bowmen against Tario's!" he cried to Jav. "Let us see a materialized battle between two mentalities."

The suggestion seemed to hearten the Lotharian, and in another moment the three stood behind solid ranks of huge bowmen who hurled taunts and menaces at the advancing company emerging from the walled city.

Jav was a new man the moment his battalions stood between him and Tario. One could almost have sworn the man believed these creatures of his strange hypnotic power to be real flesh and blood.

With hoarse battle cries they charged the bowmen of Tario. Barbed shafts flew thick and fast. Men fell, and the ground was red with gore.

Carthoris and Thuvia had difficulty in reconciling the reality of it all with their knowledge of the truth. They saw utan after utan march from the gate in perfect step to reinforce the outnumbered company which Tario had first sent forth to arrest them.

They saw Jav's forces grow correspondingly until all about them rolled a sea of fighting, cursing warriors, and the dead lay in heaps about the field.

Jav and Tario seemed to have forgotten all else beside the struggling bowmen that surged to and fro, filling the broad field between the forest and the city.

The wood loomed close behind Thuvia and Carthoris. The latter cast a glance toward Jav.

"Come!" he whispered to the girl. "Let them fight out their empty battle—neither, evidently, has power to harm the other. They are like two controversialists hurling words at one another. While they are engaged we may as well be devoting our energies to an attempt to find the passage through the cliffs to the plain beyond."

As he spoke, Jav, turning from the battle for an instant, caught his words. He saw the girl move to accompany the Heliumite. A cunning look leaped to the Lotharian's eyes.

The thing that lay beyond that look had been deep in his heart since first he had laid eyes upon Thuvia of Ptarth. He had not recognized it, however, until now that she seemed about to pass out of his existence.

He centred his mind upon the Heliumite and the girl for an instant.

Carthoris saw Thuvia of Ptarth step forward with outstretched hand. He was surprised at this sudden softening toward him, and it was with a full heart that he let his fingers close upon hers, as together they turned away from forgotten Lothar, into the woods, and bent their steps toward the distant mountains.

As the Lotharian had turned toward them, Thuvia had been surprised to hear Carthoris suddenly voice a new plan.

"Remain here with Jav," she had heard him say, "while I go to search for the passage through the cliffs."

She had dropped back in surprise and disappointment, for she knew that there was no reason why she should not have accompanied him. Certainly she should have been safer with him than left here alone with the Lotharian.

And Jav watched the two and smiled his cunning smile.

When Carthoris had disappeared within the wood, Thuvia seated herself apathetically upon the scarlet sward to watch the seemingly interminable struggles of the bowmen.

The long afternoon dragged its weary way toward darkness, and still the imaginary legions charged and re-treated. The sun was about to set when Tario commenced to withdraw his troops slowly toward the city.

His plan for cessation of hostilities through the night evidently met with Jav's entire approval, for he caused his forces to form themselves in orderly utans and march just within the edge of the wood, where they were soon busily engaged in preparing their evening meal, and spreading down their sleeping silks and furs for the night.

Thuvia could scarce repress a smile as she noted the scrupulous care with which Jav's imaginary men attended to each tiny detail of deportment as truly as if they had been real flesh and blood.

Sentries were posted between the camp and the city. Officers clanked hither and thither issuing commands and seeing to it that they were properly carried out.

Thuvia turned toward Jav.

"Why is it," she asked, "that you observe such careful nicety in the regulation of your creatures when Tario knows quite as well as you that they are but figments of your brain? Why not permit them simply to dissolve into thin air until you again require their futile service?"

"You do not understand them," replied Jav. "While they exist they are real. I do but call them into being now, and in a way direct their general actions. But there-after, until I dissolve them, they are as actual as you or I. Their officers command them, under my guidance. I am the general—that is all. And the psychological effect upon the enemy is far greater than were I to treat them merely as substanceless vagaries.

"Then, too," continued the Lotharian, "there is always the hope, which with us is little short of belief, that some day these materializations will merge into the real—that they will remain, some of them, after we have dissolved their fellows, and that thus we shall have discovered a means for perpetuating our dying race.

"Some there are who claim already to have accomplished the thing. It is generally supposed that the etherealists have quite a few among their number who are permanent materializations. It is even said that such is Tario, but that cannot be, for he existed before we had discovered the full possibilities of suggestion.

"There are others among us who insist that none of us is real. That we could not have existed all these ages without material food and water had we ourselves been material. Although I am a realist, I rather incline toward this belief myself.

"It seems well and sensibly based upon the belief that our ancient forbears developed before their extinction such wondrous mentalities that some of the stronger minds among them lived after the death of their bodies—that we are but the deathless minds of individuals long dead.

"It would appear possible, and yet in so far as I am concerned I have all the attributes of corporeal existence. I eat, I sleep"—he paused, casting a meaning look upon the girl—"I love!"

Thuvia could not mistake the palpable meaning of his words and expression. She turned away with a little shrug of disgust that was not lost upon the Lotharian.

He came close to her and seized her arm.

"Why not Jav?" he cried. "Who more honourable than the second of the world's most ancient race? Your Heliumite? He has gone. He has deserted you to your fate to save himself. Come, be Jav's!"

Thuvia of Ptarth rose to her full height, her lifted shoulder turned toward the man, her haughty chin upraised, a scornful twist to her lips.

"You lie!" she said quietly. "the Helinmite knows less of disloyalty than he knows of fear, and of fear he is as ignorant as the unhatched young."

"Then where is he?" taunted the Lotharian. "I tell you he has fled the valley. He has left you to your fate. But Jav will see that it is a pleasant one. To-morrow we shall return into Lothar at the head of my victorious army, and I shall be jeddak and you shall be my consort. Come!" And he attempted to crush her to his breast.

The girl struggled to free herself, striking at the man with her metal armlets. Yet still he drew her toward him, until both were suddenly startled by a hideous growl that rumbled from the dark wood close behind them.

CHAPTER X

KAR KOMAK, THE BOWMAN

As CARTHORIS moved through the forest toward the distant cliffs with Thuvia's hand still tight pressed in his, he wondered a little at the girl's continued silence, yet the contact of her cool palm against his was so pleasant that he feared to break the spell of her new-found reliance in him by speaking.

Onward through the dim wood they passed until the shadows of the quick coming Martian night commenced to close down upon them. Then it was that Carthoris turned to speak to the girl at his side.

They must plan together for the future. It was his idea to pass through the cliffs at once if they could locate the passage, and he was quite positive that they were now close to it; but he wanted her assent to the proposition.

As his eyes rested upon her, he was struck by her strangely ethereal appearance. She seemed suddenly to have dissolved into the tenuous substance of a dream, and as he continued to gaze upon her, she faded slowly from his sight.

For an instant he was dumbfounded, and then the whole truth flashed suddenly upon him. Jav had caused him to believe that Thuvia was accompanying him through the wood while, as a matter of fact, he had detained the girl for himself!

Carthoris was horrified. He cursed himself for his stupidity, and yet he knew that the fiendish power which the Lotharian had invoked to confuse him might have deceived any.

Scarce had he realized the truth than he had started to retrace his steps toward Lothar, but now he moved at a trot, the Earthly thews that he had inherited from his father carrying him swiftly over the soft carpet of fallen leaves and rank grass.

Thuvia's brilliant light flooded the plain before the walled city of Lothar as Carthoris broke from the wood opposite the great gate that had given the fugitives egress from the city earlier in the day.

At first he saw no indication that there was another than himself anywhere about. The plain was deserted. No myriad bowmen camped now beneath the overhanging verdure of the giant trees. No gory heaps of tortured dead defaced the beauty of the scarlet sward. All was silence. All was peace.

The Heliumite, scarce pausing at the forest's verge, pushed on across the plain toward the city, when presently he descried a huddled form in the grass at his feet.

It was the body of a man, lying prone. Carthoris turned the figure over upon its back. It was Jav, but torn and mangled almost beyond recognition.

The prince bent low to note if any spark of life remained, and as he did so the lids raised and dull, suffering eyes looked up onto his.

"The Princess of Ptarth!" cried Carthoris. "Where is she? Answer me, man, or I complete the work that another has so well begun."

"Komal," muttered Jav. "He sprang upon me . . . and would have devoured me but for the girl. Then they went away together into the wood—the girl and the great banth . . . her fingers twined in his tawny mane."

"Which way went they?" asked Carthoris.

"There," replied Jav faintly, "toward the passage through the cliffs."

The Prince of Helium waited to hear no more, but springing to his feet, raced back again into the forest.

It was dawn when he reached the mouth of the dark tunnel that would lead him to the other world beyond this valley of ghostly memories and strange hypnotic influences and menaces.

Within the long, dark passages he met with no accident or obstacle, coming at last into the light of day beyond the mountains, and no great distance from the southern verge of the domains of the Torquasians, not more than one hundred and fifty haad at the most.

From the boundary of Torquas to the city of Aaanthor is a distance of some two hundred haads, so that the Heliumite had before him a journey of more than one hundred and fifty Earth miles between him and Aaanthor.

He could at best but hazard a chance guess that toward Aaanthor Thuvia would take her flight. There lay the nearest water, and there might be expected some day a rescuing party from her father's empire; for Carthoris knew Thuvan Dihn well enough to know that he would leave no stone unturned until he had tracked down the truth as to his daughter's abduction, and learned all that there might be to learn of her whereabouts.

He realized, of course, that the trick which had laid suspicion upon him would greatly delay the discovery of the truth, but little did he guess to what vast proportions had the results of the villainy of Astok of Dusar already grown.

Even as he emerged from the mouth of the passage to look across the foothills in the direction of Aaanthor, a Ptarth battle fleet was winging its majestic way slowly toward the twin cities of Helium, while from far distant Kaol raced another mighty armada to join forces with its ally.

He did not know that in the face of the circumstantial evidence against him even his own people had commenced to entertain suspicions that he might have stolen the Ptarthian princess.

He did not know of the lengths to which the Dusarians had gone to disrupt the friendship and alliance which existed between the three great powers of the eastern hemisphere—Helium, Ptarth and Kaol.

How Dusarian emissaries had found employment in important posts in the foreign offices of the three great nations, and how, through these men, messages from one jeddak to another were altered and garbled until the patience and pride of the three rulers and former friends could no longer endure the humiliations and insults contained in these falsified papers—not any of this he knew.

Nor did he know how even to the last John Carter, Warlord of Mars, had refused to permit the jeddak of Helium to declare war against either Ptarth or Kaol, because of his implicit belief in his son, and that eventually all would be satisfactorily explained.

And now two great fleets were moving upon Helium, while the Dusarian spies at the court of Tardos Mors saw to it that the twin cities remained in ignorance of their danger.

War had been declared by Thuvan Dihn, but the messenger who had been dispatched with the proclamation had been a Dusarian who had seen to it that no word of warning reached the twin cities of the approach of a hostile fleet.

For several days diplomatic relations had been severed between Helium and her two most powerful neighbours, and with the departure of the ministers had come a total cessation of wireless communication between the disputants, as is usual upon Barsoom.

But of all this Carthoris was ignorant. All that interested him at present was the finding of Thuvia of Ptarth. Her trail beside that of the huge banth had been well marked to the tunnel, and was once more visible leading southward into the foothills.

As he followed rapidly downward toward the dead sea-bottom, where he knew he must lose the spoor in the resilient ochre vegetation, he was suddenly surprised to see a naked man approaching him from the north-east.

As the fellow drew closer, Carthoris halted to await his

coming. He knew that the man was unarmed, and that he was apparently a Lotharian, for his skin was white and his hair auburn.

He approached the Heliumite without sign of fear, and when quite close called out the cheery Barsoomian "kaor" of greeting.

"Who are you?" asked Carthoris.

"I am Kar Komak, odwar of the bowmen," replied the other. "A strange thing has happened to me. For ages Tario has been bringing me into existence as he needed the services of the army of his mind. Of all the bowmen it has been Kar Komak who has been oftenest materialized.

"For a long time Tario has been concentrating his mind upon my permanent materialization. It has been an obsession with him that some day this thing could be accomplished and the future of Lothar assured. He asserted that matter was nonexistent except in the imagination of man—that all was mental, and so he believed that by persisting in his suggestion he could eventually make of me a permanent suggestion in the minds of all creatures.

"Yesterday he succeeded, but at such a time! It must have come all unknown to him, as it came to me without my knowledge, as, with my horde of yelling bowmen, I pursued the fleeing Torquasians back to their ochre plains.

"As darkness settled and the time came for us to fade once more into thin air, I suddenly found myself alone upon the edge of the great plain which lies yonder at the foot of the low hills.

"My men were gone back to the nothingness from which they had sprung, but I remained—naked and unarmed.

"At first I could not understand, but at last came a realization of what had occurred. Tario's long suggestions had at last prevailed, and Kar Komak had become a reality in the world of men; but my harness and my weapons had faded away with my fellows, leaving me naked and unarmed in a hostile country far from Lothar."

"You wish to return to Lothar?" asked Carthoris.

"No!" replied Kar Komak quickly. "I have no love for Tario. Being a creature of his mind, I know him too well. He is cruel and tyrannical—a master I have no desire to serve. Now that he has succeeded in accomplishing my permanent materialization, he will be unbearable, and he will go on until he has filled Lothar with his creatures. I wonder if he has succeeded as well with the maid of Lothar."

"I thought there were no women there," said Carthoris.

"In a hidden apartment in the palace of Tario," replied Kar Komak, "the jeddak has maintained the suggestion of a beautiful girl, hoping that some day she would become permanent. I have seen her there. She is wonderful! But for her sake I hope that Tario succeeds not so well with her as he has with me.

"Now, red man, I have told you of myself—what of you?"

Carthoris liked the face and manner of the bowman. There has been no sign of doubt or fear in his expression as he had approached the heavily-armed Heliumite, and he had spoken directly and to the point.

So the Prince of Helium told the bowman of Lothar who he was and what adventure had brought him to this far country.

"Good!" exclaimed the other, when he had done. "Kar Komak will accompany you. Together we shall find the Princess of Ptarth and with you Kar Komak will return to the world of men—such a world as he knew in the long-gone past when the ships of mighty Lothar ploughed angry Throxus, and the roaring surf beat against the barrier of these parched and dreary hills."

"What mean you?" asked Carthoris. "Had you really a former actual existence?"

"Most assuredly," replied Kar Komak. "In my day I commanded the fleets of Lothar—mightiest of all the fleets that sailed the five salt seas.

"Wherever men lived upon Barsoom there was the name of Kar Komak known and respected. Peaceful were the land races in those distant days—only the seafarers were warriors; but now has the glory of the past faded, nor did I think until I met you that there remained upon Barsoom a single person of our own mould who lived and loved and fought as did the ancient seafarers of my time.

"Ah, but it will seem good to see men once again—real men! Never had I much respect for the landsmen of my day. They remained in their walled cities wasting their time in play, depending for their protection entirely upon the sea race. And the poor creatures who remain, the Tarios and Jaos of Lothar, are even worse than their ancient forbears."

Carthoris was a trifle sceptical as to the wisdom of permitting the stranger to attach himself to him. There was always the chance that he was but the essence of some hypnotic treachery which Tario or Jav was attempt to exert upon the Heliumite; and yet, so sincere had been the manner and the words of the bowman, so much the fighting man did he seem, but Carthoris could not find it in his heart to doubt him.

The outcome of the matter was that he gave the naked odwar leave to accompany him, and together they set out upon the spoor of Thuvia and Komal.

Down to the ochre sea-bottom the trail led. There it disappeared, as Carthoris had known that it would; but where it entered the plain its direction had been toward Aaanthor and so toward Aaanthor the two turned their faces.

It was a long and tedious journey, fraught with many dangers. The bowman could not travel at the pace set by Carthoris, whose muscles carried him with great rapidity over the face of the small planet, the force of gravity of which exerts so much less retarding power than that of the Earth. Fifty miles a day is a fair average for a Barsoomian, but the son of John Carter might easily have covered a hundred or more miles had he cared to desert his new-found comrade.

All the way they were in constant danger of discovery

by roving bands of Torquasians, and especially was this true before they reached the boundary of Torquas.

Good fortune was with them, however, and although they sighted two detachments of the savage green men, they were not themselves seen.

And so they came, upon the morning of the third day, within sight of the glistening domes of distant Aaanthor. Throughout the journey Carthoris had ever strained his eyes ahead in search of Thuvia and the great banth; but not till now had he seen aught to give him hope.

This morning, far ahead, half-way between themselves and Aaanthor, the men saw two tiny figures moving toward the city. For a moment they watched them intently. Then Carthoris, convinced, leaped forward at a rapid run, Kar Komak following as swiftly as he could.

The Heliumite shouted to attract the girl's attention, and presently he was rewarded by seeing her turn and stand looking toward him. At her side the great banth stood with up-pricked ears, watching the approaching man.

Not yet could Thuvia of Ptarth have recognized Carthoris, though that it was he she must have been convinced, for she waited there for him without sign of fear.

Presently he saw her point toward the northwest, beyond him. Without slackening his pace, he turned his eyes in the direction she indicated.

Racing silently over the thick vegetation, not half a mile behind, came a score of fierce green warriors, charging him upon their mighty thoats.

To their right was Kar Komak, naked and unarmed, yet running valiantly toward Carthoris and shouting warning as though he, too, had but just discovered the silent, menacing company that moved so swiftly forward with couched spears and ready long-swords.

Carthoris shouted to the Lotharian, warning him back, for he knew that he could but uselessly sacrifice his life by placing himself, all unarmed, in the path of the cruel and relentless savages.

But Kar Komak never hesitated. With shouts of encouragement to his new friend, he hurried onward toward the Prince of Helium. The red man's heart leaped in response to this exhibition of courage and self-sacrifice. He regretted now that he had not thought to give Kar Komak one of his swords; but it was too late to attempt it, for should he wait for the Lotharian to overtake him or return to meet him, the Torquasians would reach Thuvia of Ptarth before he could do so.

Even as it was, it would be nip and tuck as to who came first to her side.

Again he turned his face in her direction, and now, from Aaanthor way, he saw a new force hastening toward them—two medium-sized war craft—and even at the distance they still were from him he discerned the device of Dusar upon their bows.

Now, indeed, seemed little hope for Thuvia of Ptarth. With savage warriors of the hordes of Torquas charging toward her from one direction, and no less implacable enemies, in the form of the creatures of Astok, Prince of Dusar, bearing down upon her from another, while only a banth, a red warrior, and an unarmed bowman were near to defend her, her plight was quite hopeless and her cause already lost ere ever it was contested.

As Thuvia saw Carthoris approaching, she felt again that unaccountable sensation of entire relief from responsibility and fear that she had experienced upon a former occasion. Nor could she account for it while her mind still tried to convince her heart that the Prince of Helium had been instrumental in her abduction from her father's court. She only knew that she was glad when he was by her side, and that with him there all things seemed possible—even such impossible things as escape from her present predicament.

Now had he stopped, panting, before her. A brave smile of encouragement lit his face.

"Courage, my princess," he whispered.

To the girl's memory flashed the occasion upon which he had used those same words—in the throne-room of

Tario of Lothar as they had commenced to slip down the sinking marble floor toward an unknown fate.

Then she had not chidden him for the use of that familiar salutation, nor did she chide him now, though she was promised to another. She wondered at herself—flushing at her own turpitude; for upon Barsoom it is a shameful thing for a woman to listen to those two words from another than her husband or her betrothed.

Carthoris saw her flush of mortification, and in an instant regretted his words. There was but a moment before the green warriors would be upon them.

"Forgive me!" said the man in a low voice. "Let my great love be my excuse—that, and the belief that I have but a moment more of life," and with the words he turned to meet the foremost of the green warriors.

The fellow was charging with couched spear, but Carthoris leaped to one side, and as the great thoat and its rider hurtled harmlessly past him he swung his longsword in a mighty cut that clove the green carcass in twain.

At the same moment Kar Komak leaped with bare hands clawing at the leg of another of the huge riders; the balance of the horde raced in to close quarters, dismounting the better to wield their favourite long-swords; the Dusarian fliers touched the soft carpet of the ochre-clad sea-bottom, disgorging fifty fighting men from their bowels; and into the swirling sea of cutting, slashing swords sprang Komal, the great banth.

CHAPTER XI

GREEN MEN AND WHITE APES

A TORQUASIAN SWORD smote a glancing blow across the forehead of Carthoris. He had a fleeting vision of soft arms about his neck, and warm lips close to his before he lost consciousness.

How long he lay there senseless he could not guess; but when he opened his eyes again he was alone, except for the bodies of the dead green men and Dusarians, and the carcass of a great banth that lay half across his own.

Thuvia was gone, nor was the body of Kar Komak among the dead.

Weak from loss of blood, Carthoris made his way slowly toward Aaanthor, reaching its outskirts at dark.

He wanted water more than any other thing, and so he kept on up a broad avenue toward the great central plaza, where he knew the precious fluid was to be found in a half-ruined building opposite the great palace of the ancient jeddak, who once had ruled this mighty city.

Disheartened and discouraged by the strange sequence of events that seemed fore-ordained to thwart his every attempt to serve the Princess of Ptarth, he paid little or no attention to his surroundings, moving through the deserted city as though no great white apes lurked in the black shadows of the mystery-haunted piles that flanked the broad avenues and the great plaza.

But if Carthoris was careless of his surroundings, not so other eyes that watched his entrance into the plaza, and followed his slow footsteps toward the marble pile that housed the tiny, half-choked spring whose water one might gain only by scratching a deep hole in the red sand that covered it.

And as the Heliumite entered the small building a dozen mighty, grotesque figures emerged from the doorway of the palace to speed noiselessly across the plaza toward him.

For half an hour Carthoris remained in the building, digging for water and gaining the few much-needed drops which were the fruits of his labour. Then he rose and slowly left the structure. Scarce had he stepped beyond the threshold than twelve Torquasian warriors leaped upon him.

No time then to draw long-sword; but swift from his harness flew his long, slim dagger, and as he went down beneath them more than a single green heart ceased beating at the bite of that keen point.

Then they overpowered him and took his weapons away; but only nine of the twelve warriors who had crossed the plaza returned with their prize.

They dragged their prisoner roughly to the palace pits, where in utter darkness they chained him with rusty links to the solid masonry of the wall.

"To-morrow Thar Ban will speak with you," they said. "Now he sleeps. But great will be his pleasure when he learns who has wandered amongst us—and great will be the pleasure of Hortan Gur when Thar Ban drags before him the mad fool who dared prick the great jeddak with his sword."

Then they left him to the silence and the darkness.

For what seemed hours Carthoris squatted upon the stone floor of his prison, his back against the wall in which was sunk the heavy eye-bolt that secured the chain which held him.

Then, from out the mysterious blackness before him, there came to his ears the sound of naked feet moving stealthily upon stone—approaching nearer and nearer to where he lay, unarmed and defenceless.

Minutes passed—minutes that seemed hours—during which time periods of sepulchral silence would be followed by a repetition of the uncanny scraping of naked feet slinking warily upon him.

At last he heard a sudden rush of unshod soles across the empty blackness, and at a little distance a scuffling sound, heavy breathing, and once what he thought the muttered imprecation of a man battling against great odds. Then the clanging of a chain, and a noise as of the snapping back against stone of a broken link.

Again came silence. But for a moment only. Now he heard once more the soft feet approaching him. He thought that he discerned wicked eyes gleaming fearfully at him through the darkness. He knew that he could hear the heavy breathing of powerful lungs.

Then came the rush of many feet toward him, and the *things* were upon him.

Hands terminating in manlike fingers clutched at his throat and arms and legs. Hairy bodies strained and struggled against his own smooth hide as he battled in grim silence against these horried foemen in the darkness of the pits of ancient Aaanthor.

Thewed like some giant god was Carthoris of Helium, yet in the clutches of these unseen creatures of the pit's Stygian night he was helpless as a frail woman.

Yet he battled on, striking futile blows against great, hispid breasts he could not see; feeling thick, squat throats beneath his fingers; the drool of saliva upon his cheek, and hot, foul breath in his nostrils.

Fangs, too, mighty fangs, he knew were close, and why they did not sink into his flesh he could not guess.

At last he became aware of the mighty surging of a number of his antagonists back and forth upon the great chain that held him, and presently came the same sound that he had heard at a little distance from him a short time before he had been attacked—his chain had parted and the broken end snapped back against the stone wall.

Now he was seized upon either side and dragged at a rapid pace through the dark corridors—toward what fate he could not even guess.

At first he had thought his foes might be of the tribe of Torquas, but their hairy bodies belied that belief. Now he was at last quite sure of their identity, though why they had not killed and devoured him at once he could not imagine.

After half an hour or more of rapid racing through the underground passages that are a distinguishing feature of all Barsoomian cities, modern as well as ancient, his captors suddenly emerged into the moonlight of a courtyard, far from the central plaza.

Immediately Carthoris saw that he was in the power of a tribe of the great white apes of Barsoom. All that had caused him doubt before as to the identity of his attackers was the hairiness of their breasts, for the white apes are entirely hairless except for a great shock bristling from their heads.

Now he saw the cause of that which had deceived him—across the chest of each of them were strips of hairy hide, usually of banth, in imitation of the harness of the green warriors who so often camped at their deserted city.

Carthoris had read of the existence of tribes of apes that seemed to be progressing slowly toward higher standards of intelligence. Into the hands of such, he realized, he had fallen; but—what were their intentions toward him?

As he glanced about the courtyard, he saw fully fifty of the hideous beasts, squatting on their haunches, and at a little distance from him another human being, closely guarded.

As his eyes met those of his fellow-captive a smile lit the other's face, and: "Kaor, red man!" burst from his lips. It was Kar Komak, the bowman.

"Kaor!" cried Carthoris, in response. "How came you here, and what befell the princess?"

"Red men like yourself descended in mighty ships that sailed the air, even as the great ships of my distant day sailed the five seas," replied Kar Komak. "They fought with the green men of Torquas. They slew Komal, god of Lothar. I thought they were your friends, and I was glad when finally those of them who survived the battle carried the red girl to one of the ships and sailed away with her into the safety of the high air.

"Then the green men seized me, and carried me to a great, empty city, where they chained me to a wall in a black pit. Afterward came these and dragged me hither. And what of you, red man?"

Carthoris related all that had befallen him, and as the two men talked the great apes squatted about them watching them intently.

"What are we to do now?" asked the bowman.

"Our case looks rather hopeless," replied Carthoris ruefully. "These creatures are born man-eaters. Why they have not already devoured us I cannot imagine—there!" he whispered. "See? The end is coming."

Kar Komak looked in the direction Carthoris indicated to see a huge ape advancing with a mighty bludgeon.

"It is thus they like best to kill their prey," said Carthoris.

"Must we die without a struggle?" asked Kar Komak.

"Not I," replied Carthoris, "though I know how futile our best defence must be against these mighty brutes! Oh, for a long-sword!"

"Or a good bow," added Kar Komak, "and a utan of bowmen."

At the words Carthoris half sprang to his feet, only to be dragged roughly down by his guard.

"Kar Komak!" he cried. "Why cannot you do what Tario and Jav did? They had no bowmen other than those of their own creation. You must know the secret of their power. Call forth your own utan, Kar Komak!"

The Lotharian looked at Carthoris in wide-eyed astonishment as the full purport of the suggestion bore in upon his understanding.

"Why not?" he murmured.

The savage ape bearing the mighty bludgeon was slinking toward Carthoris. The Heliumite's fingers were working as he kept his eyes upon his executioner. Kar Komak bent his gaze penetratingly upon the apes. The effort of his mind was evidenced in the sweat upon his contracted brows.

The creature that was to slay the red man was almost within arm's reach of his prey when Carthoris heard a hoarse shout from the opposite side of the courtyard. In common with the squatting apes and the demon with the club he turned in the direction of the sound, to see a company of sturdy bowmen rushing from the doorway of a near-by building.

With screams of rage the apes leaped to their feet to meet the charge. A volley of arrows met them half-way, sending a dozen rolling lifeless to the ground. Then the apes closed with their adversaries. All their attention was occupied by the attackers—even the guard had deserted the prisoners to join in the battle.

"Come!" whispered Kar Komak. "Now may we escape while their attention is diverted from us by my bowmen."

"And leave those brave fellows leaderless?" cried Carthoris, whose loyal nature revolted at the merest suggestion of such a thing.

Kar Komak laughed.

"You forget," he said, "that they are but thin air—figments of my brain. They will vanish, unscathed, when we have no further need for them. Praised be your first ancestor, redman, that you thought of this chance in time! It would never have occurred to me to imagine that I might wield the same power that brought me into existence."

"You are right," said Carthoris. "Still, I hate to leave them, though there is naught else to do," and so the two turned from the courtyard, and making their way into one of the broad avenues, crept stealthily in the shadows of the building toward the great central plaza upon which were the buildings occupied by the green warriors when they visited the deserted city.

When they had come to the plaza's edge Carthoris halted.

"Wait here," he whispered. "I go to fetch thoats, since on foot we may never hope to escape the clutches of these green fiends."

To reach the courtyard where the thoats were kept it was necessary for Carthoris to pass through one of the buildings which surrounded the square. Which were occupied and which not he could not even guess, so he was compelled to take considerable chances to gain the enclosure in which he could hear the restless beasts squealing and quarrelling among themselves.

Chance carried him through a dark doorway into a large chamber in which lay a score or more green warriors wrapped in their sleeping silks and furs. Scarce had Carthoris passed through the short hallway that connected the door of the building and the great room beyond it than he became aware of the presence of something or some one in the hallway through which he had but just passed.

He heard a man yawn, and then, behind him, he saw the figure of a sentry rise from where the fellow had been dozing, and stretching himself resume his wakeful watchfulness.

Carthoris realized that he must have passed within a foot of the warrior, doubtless rousing him from his slumber. To retreat now would be impossible. Yet to cross through that roomful of sleeping warriors seemed almost equally beyond the pale of possibility.

Carthoris shrugged his broad shoulders and chose the lesser evil. Warily he entered the room. At his right, against the wall, leaned several swords and rifles and spears—extra weapons which the warriors had stacked here ready to their hands should there be a night alarm calling them suddenly from slumber. Beside each sleeper lay his weapon—these were never far from their owners from childhood to death.

The sight of the swords made the young man's palm itch. He stepped quickly to them, selecting two short-swords—one for Kar Komak, the other for himself; also some trappings for his naked comrade.

Then he started directly across the centre of the apart-ment among the sleeping Torquasians.

Not a man of them moved until Carthoris had com-pleted more than half of the short though dangerous journey. Then a fellow directly in his path turned rest-lessly upon his sleeping silks and furs.

The Heliumite paused above him, one of the short-swords in readiness should the warrior awaken. For what seemed an eternity to the young prince the green man continued to move uneasily upon his couch, then, as though actuated by springs, he leaped to his feet and faced the red man.

Instantly Carthoris struck, but not before a savage grunt escaped the other's lips. In an instant the room was in turmoil. Warriors leaped to their feet, grasping their weapons as they rose, and shouting to one another for an explanation of the disturbance.

To Carthoris all within the room was plainly visible in the dim light reflected from without, for the further moon stood directly at zenith; but to the eyes of the newly-awakened green men objects as yet had not taken on familiar forms—they but saw vaguely the figures of warriors moving about their apartment.

Now one stumbled against the corpse of him whom Carthoris had slain. The fellow stooped and his hand came in contact with the cleft skull. He saw about him the giant figures of other green men, and so he jumped to the only conclusion that was open to him.

"The Thurds!" he cried. "The Thurds are upon us! Rise, warriors of Torquas, and drive home your swords within the hearts of Torquas' ancient enemies!"

Instantly the green men began to fall upon one an-other with naked swords. Their savage lust of battle was aroused. To fight, to kill, to die with cold steel buried in their vitals! Ah, that to them was Nirvana.

Carthoris was quick to guess their error and take advantage of it. He knew that in the pleasure of killing they might fight on long after they had discovered their mistake, unless their attention was distracted by sight of the real cause of the altercation, and so he lost no time in continuing across the room to the doorway upon the opposite side, which opened into the inner court, where the savage thoats were squealing and fighting among themselves.

Once here he had no easy task before him. To catch and mount one of these habitually rageful and intractable beasts was no child's play under the best of conditions; but now, when silence and time were such important considerations, it might well have seemed quite hopeless to a less resourceful and optimistic man than the son of the great warlord.

From his father he had learned much concerning the traits of these mighty beasts, and from Tars Tarkas, also, when he had visited that great green jeddak among his horde at Thark. So now he centred upon the work in hand all that he had ever learned about them from others and from his own experience, for he, too, had ridden and handled them many times.

The temper of the thoats of Torquas appeared even shorter than their vicious cousins among the Tharks and Warhoons, and for a time it seemed unlikely that he should escape a savage charge on the part of a couple of old bulls that circled, squealing, about him; but at last he managed to get close enough to one of them to touch the beast. With the feel of his hand upon the sleek hide the creature quieted, and in answer to the telepathic command of the red man sank to its knees.

In a moment Carthoris was upon its back, guiding it toward the great gate that leads from the courtyard through a large building at one end into an avenue beyond.

The other bull, still squealing and enraged, followed

after his fellow. There was no bridle upon either, for
these strange creatures are controlled entirely by suggestion—when they are controlled at all.

Even in the hands of the giant green men bridle reins
would be hopelessly futile against the mad savagery and
mastodonic strength of the thoat, and so they are guided
by that strange telepathic power with which the men
of Mars have learned to communicate in a crude way
with the lower orders of their planet.

With difficulty Carthoris urged the two beasts to the
gate, where, leaning down, he raised the latch. Then the
thoat that he was riding placed his great shoulder to
the skeel-wood planking, pushed through, and a moment
later the man and the two beasts were swinging silently
down the avenue to the edge of the plaza, where Kar
Komak hid.

Here Carthoris found considerable difficulty in sub-
duing the second thoat, and as Kar Komak had never
before ridden one of the beasts, it seemed a most hopeless job; but at last the bowman managed to scramble
to the sleek back, and again the two beasts fled softly
down the moss-grown avenues toward the open sea-
bottom beyond the city.

All that night and the following day and the second
night they rode toward the north-east. No indication of
pursuit developed, and at dawn of the second day Carthoris saw in the distance the waving ribbon of great
trees that marked one of the long Barsoomian waterways.

Immediately they abandoned their thoats and approached the cultivated district on foot. Carthoris also
discarded the metal from his harness, or such of it as
might serve to identify him as a Heliumite, or of royal
blood, for he did not know to what nation belonged this
waterway, and upon Mars it is always well to assume
every man and nation your enemy until you have
learned the contrary.

It was mid-forenoon when the two at last entered
one of the roads that cut through the cultivated districts

at regular intervals, joining the arid wastes on either side with the great, white, central highway that follows through the centre from end to end of the far-reaching, threadlike farm lands.

The high wall surrounding the fields served as a protection against surprise by raiding green hordes, as well as keeping the savage banths and other carnivora from the domestic animals and the human beings upon the farms.

Carthoris stopped before the first gate he came to, pounding for admission. The young man who answered his summons greeted the two hospitably, though he looked with considerable wonder upon the white skin and auburn hair of the bowman.

After he had listened for a moment to a partial narration of their escape from the Torquasians, he invited them within, took them to his house and bade the servants there prepare food for them.

As they waited in the low-ceiled, pleasant livingroom of the farmhouse until the meal should be ready, Carthoris drew his host into conversation that he might learn his nationality, and thus the nation under whose dominion lay the waterway where circumstance had placed him.

"I am Halvas," said the young man, " son of Vas Kor, of Dusar, a noble in the retinue of Astok, Prince of Dusar. At present I am Dwar of the Road for this district."

Carthoris was very glad that he had not disclosed his identity, for though he had no idea of anything that had transpired since he had left Helium, or that Astok was at the bottom of all his misfortunes, he well knew that the Dusarian had no love for him, and that he could hope for no assistance within the dominions of Dusar.

"And who are you?" asked Hal Vas. "By your appearance I take you for a fighting man, but I see no insignia upon your harness. Can it be that you are a panthan?"

Now, these wandering soldiers of fortune are common upon Barsoom, where most men love to fight. They sell their services wherever war exists, and in the occasional brief intervals when there is no organized warfare between the red nations, they join one of the numerous expeditions that are constantly being dispatched against the green men in protection of the waterways that traverse the wilder portions of the globe.

When their service is over they discard the metal of the nation they have been serving until they shall have found a new master. In the intervals they wear no insignia, their war-worn harness and grim weapons being sufficient to attest their calling.

The suggestion was a happy one, and Carthoris embraced the chance it afforded to account satisfactorily for himself. There was, however, a single drawback. In times of war such panthans as happened to be within the domain of a belligerent nation were compelled to don the insignia of that nation and fight with her warriors.

As far as Carthoris knew Dusar was not at war with any other nation, but there was never any telling when one red nation would be flying at the throat of a neighbour, even though the great and powerful alliance at the head of which was his father, John Carter, had managed to maintain a long peace upon the greater portion of Barsoom.

A pleasant smile lighted Hal Vas' face as Carthoris admitted his vocation.

"It is well," exclaimed the young man, "that you chanced to come hither, for here you will find the means of obtaining service in short order. My father, Vas Kor, is even now with me, having come hither to recruit a force for the new war against Helium."

CHAPTER XII

TO SAVE DUSAR

THUVIA OF PTARTH, battling for more than life against the lust of Jav, cast a quick glance over her shoulder toward the forest from which had rumbled the fierce growl. Jav looked, too.

What they saw filled each with apprehension. It was Komal, the banth-god, rushing wide-jawed upon them!

Which had he chosen for his prey? Or was it to be both?

They had not long to wait, for though the Lotharian attempted to hold the girl between himself and the terrible fangs, the great beast found him at last.

Then, shrieking, he attempted to fly toward Lothar, after pushing Thuvia bodily into the face of the maneater. But his flight was of short duration. In a moment Komal was upon him, rending his throat and chest with demoniacal fury.

The girl reached their side a moment later, but it was with difficulty that she tore the mad beast from its prey. Still growling and casting hungry glances back upon Jav, the banth at last permitted itself to be led away into the wood.

With her giant protector by her side Thuvia set forth to find the passage through the cliffs, that she might attempt the seemingly impossible feat of reaching far-

distant Ptarth across the more than seventeen thousand
haads of savage Barsoom.

She could not believe that Carthoris had deliberately
deserted her, and so she kept a constant watch for him;
but as she bore too far to the north in her search for
the tunnel she passed the Heliumite as he was returning
to Lothar in search of her.

Thuvia of Ptarth was having difficulty in determining
the exact status of the Prince of Helium in her heart.
She could not admit even to herself that she loved him,
and yet she had permitted him to apply to her that
term of endearment and possession to which a Barsoomian maid should turn deaf ears when voiced by other
lips than those of her husband or fiancé—"my princess."

Kulan Tith, Jeddak of Kaol, to whom she was
affianced, commanded her respect and admiration. Had
it been that she had surrendered to her father's wishes
because of pique that the handsome Heliumite had not
taken advantage of his visits to her father's court to
push the suit for her hand that she had been quite
sure he had contemplated since that distant day the two
had sat together upon the carved seat within the gorgeous Garden of the Jeddaks that graced the inner courtyard of the palace of Salensus Oll at Kadabra?

Did she love Kulan Tith? Bravely she tried to believe that she did; but all the while her eyes wandered
through the coming darkness for the figure of a clean-
limbed fighting man—black-haired and grey-eyed. Black
was the hair of Kulan Tith; but his eyes were brown.

It was almost dark when she found the entrance to
the tunnel. Safely she passed through to the hills beyond, and here, under the bright light of Mars' two
moons, she halted to plan her future action.

Should she wait here in the hope that Carthoris
would return in search of her? Or should she continue
her way north-east toward Ptarth? Where, first, would
Carthoris have gone after leaving the valley of Lothar?

Her parched throat and dry tongue gave her the answer—toward Aaanthor and water. Well, she, too, would

go first to Aaanthor, where she might find more than
the water she needed.

With Komal by her side she felt little fear, for he
would protect her from all other savage beasts. Even
the great white apes would flee the mighty banth in
terror. Men only need she fear, but she must take this
and many other chances before she could hope to reach
her father's court again.

When at last Carthoris found her, only to be struck
down by the long-sword of a green man, Thuvia prayed
that the same fate might overtake her.

The sight of the red warriors leaping from their fliers
had, for a moment, filled her with renewed hope—
hope that Carthoris of Helium might be only stunned and
that they would rescue him; but when she saw the Dusarian metal upon their harness, and that they sought only
to escape with her alone from the charging Torquasians,
she gave up.

Komal, too, was dead—dead across the body of the
Heliumite. She was, indeed, alone now. There was
none to protect her.

The Dusarian warriors dragged her to the deck of the
nearest flier. All about them the green warriors surged in
an attempt to wrest her from the red.

At last those who had not died in the conflict gained
the decks of the two craft. The engines throbbed and
purred—the propellers whirred. Quickly the swift boats
shot heavenward.

Thuvia of Ptarth glanced about her. A man stood near,
smiling down into her face. With a gasp of recognition
she looked full into his eyes, and then with a little
moan of terror and understanding she buried her face in
her hands and sank to the polished skeel-wood deck. It
was Astok, Prince of Dusar, who bent above her.

Swift were the fliers of Astok of Dusar, and great the
need for reaching his father's court as quickly as possible,
for the fleets of war of Helium and Ptarth and Kaol were
scattered far and wide above Barsoom. Nor would it go
well with Astok or Dusar should any one of them dis-

cover Thuvia of Ptarth a prisoner upon his own vessel.

Aaanthor lies in fifty south latitude, and forty east of Horz, the deserted seat of ancient Barsoomian culture and learning, while Dusar lies fifteen degrees north of the equator and twenty degrees east from Horz.

Great though the distance is, the fliers covered it without a stop. Long before they had reached their destination Thuvia of Ptarth had learned several things that cleared up the doubts that had assailed her mind for many days. Scarce had they risen above Aaanthor than she recognized one of the crew as a member of the crew of that other flier that had borne her from her father's gardens to Aaanthor. The presence of Astok upon the craft settled the whole question. She had been stolen by emissaries of the Dusarian prince—Carthoris of Helium had had nothing to do with it.

Nor did Astok deny the charge when she accused him. He only smiled and pleaded his lo e for her.

"I would sooner mate with a white ape!" she cried, when he would have urged his suit.

Astok glowered sullenly upon her.

"You shall mate with me, Thuvia of Ptarth," he growled, "or, by your first ancestor, you shall have your preference—and mate with a white ape."

The girl made no reply, nor could he draw her into conversation during the balance of the journey.

As a matter of fact Astok was a trifle awed by the proportions of the conflict which his abduction of the Ptarthian princess had induced, nor was he over comfortable with the weight of responsibility which the possession of such a prisoner entailed.

His one thought was to get her to Dusar, and there let his father assume the responsibility. In the meantime he would be as careful as possible to do nothing to affront her, lest they all might be captured and he have to account for his treatment of the girl to one of the great jeddaks whose interest centered in her.

And so at last they came to Dusar, where Astok hid his prisoner in a secret room high in the east tower of his own palace. He had sworn his men to silence in the matter of the identity of the girl, for until he had seen his father, Nutus, Jeddak of Dusar, he dared not let any one know whom he had brought with him from the south.

But when he appeared in the great audience chamber before the cruel-lipped man who was his sire, he found his courage oozing, and he dared not speak of the princess hid within his palace. It occurred to him to test his father's sentiments upon the subject, and so he told a tale of capturing one who claimed to know the whereabouts of Thuvia of Ptarth.

"And if you command it, Sire," he said, "I will go and capture her—fetching her here to Dusar."

Nutus frowned and shook his head.

"You have done enough already to set Ptarth and Kaol and Helium all three upon us at once should they learn your part in the theft of the Ptarth princess. That you succeeded in shifting the guilt upon the Prince of Helium was fortunate, and a masterly move of strategy; but were the girl to know the truth and ever return to her father's court, all Dusar would have to pay the penalty, and to have her here a prisoner amongst us would be an admission of guilt from the consequences of which naught could save us. It would cost me my throne, Astok, and that I have no mind to lose.

"If we had her here——" the elder man suddenly commenced to muse, repeating the phrase again and again. "If we had her here, Astok," he exclaimed fiercely. "Ah, if we but had her here and none knew that she was here! Can you not guess, man? The guilt of Dusar might be for ever buried with her bones," he concluded in a low, savage whisper.

Astok, Prince of Dusar, shuddered.

Weak he was; yes, and wicked, too; but the suggestion that his father's words implied turned him cold with horror.

Cruel to their enemies are the men of Mars; but the word "enemies" is commonly interpreted to mean men only. Assassination runs riot in the great Barsoomian cities; yet to murder a woman is a crime so unthinkable that even the most hardened of the paid assassins would shrink from you in horror should you suggest such a thing to him.

Nutus was apparently oblivious to his son's all-too-patent terror at his suggestion. Presently he continued:

"You say that you know where the girl lies hid, since she was stolen from your people at Aaanthor. Should she be found by any one of the three powers, her unsupported story would be sufficient to turn them all against us.

"There is but one way, Astok," cried the older man. "You must return at once to her hiding-place and fetch her hither in all secrecy. And, look you here! Return not to Dusar without her, upon pain of death!"

Astok, Prince of Dusar, well knew his royal father's temper. He knew that in the tyrant's heart there pulsed no single throb of love for any creature.

Astok's mother had been a slave woman. Nutus had never loved her. He had never loved another. In youth he had tried to find a bride at the courts of several of his powerful neighbours, but their women would have none of him.

After a dozen daughters of his own nobility had sought self-destruction rather than wed him he had given up. And then it had been that he had legally wed one of his slaves that he might have a son to stand among the jeds when Nutus died and a new jeddak was chosen.

Slowly Astok withdrew from the presence of his father. With white face and shaking limbs he made his way to his own palace. As he crossed the courtyard his glance chanced to wander to the great east tower looming high against the azure of the sky.

At sight of it beads of sweat broke out upon his brow.

Issus! No other hand than his could be trusted to do the horrid thing. With his own fingers he must crush the life from that perfect throat, or plunge the silent blade into the red, red heart.

Her heart! The heart that he had hoped would brim with love for him!

But had it done so? He recalled the haughty contempt with which his protestations of love had been received. He went cold and then hot to the memory of it. His compunctions cooled as the self-satisfaction of a near revenge crowded out the finer instincts that had for a moment asserted themselves—the good that he had inherited from the slave woman was once again submerged in the bad blood that had come down to him from his royal sire; as, in the end, it always was.

A cold smile supplanted the terror that had dilated his eyes. He turned his steps toward the tower. He would see her before he set out upon the journey that was to blind his father to the fact that the girl was already in Dusar.

Quietly he passed in through the secret way, ascending a spiral runway to the apartment in which the Princess of Ptarth was immured.

As he entered the room he saw the girl leaning upon the sill of the east casement, gazing out across the roof tops of Dusar toward distant Ptarth. He hated Ptarth. The thought of it filled him with rage. Why not finish her now and have it done with?

At the sound of his step she turned quickly toward him. Ah, how beautiful she was! His sudden determination faded beneath the glorious light of her wondrous beauty. He would wait until he had returned from his little journey of deception—maybe there might be some other way then. Some other hand to strike the blow—with that face, with those eyes before him, he could never do it. Of that he was positive. He had always gloried in the cruelty of his nature, but, Issus! he was not that cruel. No, another must be found—one whom he could trust.

He was still looking at her as she stood there before him meeting his gaze steadily and unafraid. He felt the hot passion of his love mounting higher and higher.

Why not sue once more? If she would relent, all might yet be well. Even if his father could not be persuaded they could fly to Ptarth, laying all the blame of the knavery

and intrigue that had thrown four great nations into war,
upon the shoulders of Nutus. And who was there that
would doubt the justice of the charge?

"Thuvia," he said, "I come once again, for the last
time, to lay my heart at your feet. Ptarth and Kaol and
Dusar are battling with Helium because of you. Wed
me, Thuvia, and all may yet be as it should be."

The girl shook her head.

"Wait!" he commanded, before she could speak.
"Know the truth before you speak words that may seal,
not only your own fate, but that of the thousands of warriors who battle because of you.

"Refuse to wed me willingly, and Dusar would be laid
waste should ever the truth be known to Ptarth and Kaol
and Helium. They would raze our cities, leaving not one
stone upon another. They would scatter our peoples
across the face of Barsoom from the frozen north to the
frozen south, hunting them down and slaying them,
until this great nation remained only as a hated memory
in the minds of men.

"But while they are exterminating the Dusarians,
countless thousands of their own warriors must perish—
and all because of the stubbornness of a single woman
who would not wed the prince who loves her.

"Refuse, Thuvia of Ptarth, and there remains but a single alternative—no man must ever know your fate. Only a
handful of loyal servitors besides my royal father and
myself know that you were stolen from the gardens of
Thuvan Dihn by Astok, Prince of Dusar, or that to-day
you be imprisoned in my palace.

"Refuse, Thuvia of Ptarth, and you must die to save
Dusar—there is no other way. Nutus, the jeddak, has
so decreed. I have spoken."

For a long moment the girl let her level gaze rest full
upon the face of Astok of Dusar. Then she spoke, and
though the words were few, the unimpassioned tone carried unfathomable depths of cold contempt.

"Better all that you have threatened," she said, "than
you."

Then she turned her back upon him and went to stand once more before the east window, gazing with sad eyes toward distant Ptarth.

Astok wheeled and left the room, returning after a short interval of time with food and drink.

"Here," he said, "is sustenance until I return again. The next to enter this apartment will be your executioner. Commend yourself to your ancestors, Thuvia of Ptarth, for within a few days you shall be with them."

Then he was gone.

Half an hour later he was interviewing an officer high in the navy of Dusar.

"Whither went Vas Kor?" he asked. "He is not at his palace."

"South, to the great waterway that skirts Torquas," replied the other. "His son, Hal Vas, is Dwar of the Road there, and thither has Vas Kor gone to enlist recruits among the workers on the farms."

"Good," said Astok, and a half-hour more found him rising above Dusar in his swiftest flier.

CHAPTER XIII

TURJUN, THE PANTHAN

THE FACE OF Carthoris of Helium gave no token of the emotions that convulsed him inwardly as he heard from the lips of Hal Vas that Helium was at war with Dusar, and that fate had thrown him into the service of the enemy.

That he might utilize this opportunity to the good of Helium scarce sufficed to outweigh the chagrin he felt that he was not fighting in the open at the head of his own loyal troops.

To escape the Dusarians might prove an easy matter; and then again it might not. Should they suspect his loyalty (and the loyalty of an impressed panthan was always open to suspicion), he might not find an opportunity to elude their vigilance until after the termination of the war, which might occur within days, or, again, only after long and weary years of bloodshed.

He recalled that history recorded wars in which actual military operations had been carried on without cessation for five or six hundred years, and even now there were nations upon Barsoom with which Helium had made no peace within the history of man.

The outlook was not cheering. He could not guess that within a few hours he would be blessing the fate that had thrown him into the service of Dusar.

"Ah!" exclaimed Hal Vas. "Here is my father now.

Kaor! Vas Kor. Here is one you will be glad to meet—a doughty panthan——" He hesitated.

"Turjun," interjected Carthoris, seizing upon the first appellation that occurred to him.

As he spoke his eyes crossed quickly to the tall warrior who was entering the room. Where before had he seen that giant figure, that taciturn countenance, and the livid sword-cut from temple to mouth?

"Vas Kor," repeated Carthoris mentally. "Vas Kor!" Where had he seen the man before?

And then the noble spoke, and like a flash it all came back to Carthoris—the forward servant upon the landing-stage at Ptarth that time that he had been explaining the intricacies of his new compass to Thuvan Dihn; the lone slave that had guarded his own hangar that night he had left upon his ill-fated journey for Ptarth—the journey that had brought him so mysteriously to far Aaanthor.

"Vas Kor," he repeated aloud, "blessed be your ancestors for this meeting," nor did the Dusarian guess the wealth of meaning that lay beneath that hackneyed phrase with which a Barsoomian acknowledges an introduction.

"And blessed be yours, Turjun," replied Vas Kor.

Now came the introduction of Kar Komak to Vas Kor, and as Carthoris went through the little ceremony there came to him the only explanation he might make to account for the white skin and auburn hair of the bowman; for he feared that the truth might not be believed and thus suspicion be cast upon them both from the beginning.

"Kar Komak," he explained, "is, as you can see, a thern. He has wandered far from his icebound southern temples in search of adventure. I came upon him in the pits of Aaanthor; but though I have known him so short a time, I can vouch for his bravery and loyalty."

Since the destruction of the fabric of their false religion by John Carter, the majority of the therns had gladly accepted the new order of things, so that it was now no longer uncommon to see them mingling with the multitudes of red men in any of the great cities of the outer world, so Vas Kor neither felt nor expressed any great astonishment.

All during the interview Carthoris watched, catlike, for some indication that Vas Kor recognized in the battered panthan the erstwhile gorgeous Prince of Helium; but the sleepless nights, the long days of marching and fighting, the wounds and the dried blood had evidently sufficed to obliterate the last remnant of his likeness to his former self; and then Vas Kor had seen him but twice in all his life. Little wonder that he did not know him.

During the evening Vas Kor announced that on the morrow they should depart north toward Dusar, picking up recruits at various stations along the way.

In a great field behind the house a flier lay—a fair-sized cruiser-transport that would accommodate many men, yet swift and well armed also. Here Carthoris slept, and Kar Komak, too, with the other recruits, under guard of the regular Dusarian warriors that manned the craft.

Toward midnight Vas Kor returned to the vessel from his son's house, repairing at once to his cabin. Carthoris, with one of the Dusarians, was on watch. It was with difficulty that the Heliumite repressed a cold smile as the noble passed within a foot of him—within a foot of the long, slim, Heliumitic blade that swung in his harness.

How easy it would have been! How easy to avenge the cowardly trick that had been played upon him—to avenge Helium and Ptarth and Thuvia!

But his hand moved not toward the dagger's hilt, for first Vas Kor must serve a better purpose—he might know where Thuvia of Ptarth lay hidden now, if it had truly been Dusarians that had spirited her away during the fight before Aaanthor.

And then, too, there was the instigator of the entire foul plot. *He* must pay the penalty; and who better than Vas Kor could lead the Prince of Helium to Astok of Dusar?

Faintly out of the night there came to Carthoris's ears

the purring of a distant motor. He scanned the heavens.

Yes, there it was far in the north, dimly outlined against the dark void of space that stretched illimitably beyond it, the faint suggestion of a flier passing, unlighted, through the Barsoomian night.

Carthoris, knowing not whether the craft might be friend or foe of Dusar, gave no sign that he had seen, but turned his eyes in another direction, leaving the matter to the Dusarian who stood watch with him.

Presently the fellow discovered the oncoming craft, and sounded the low alarm which brought the balance of the watch and an officer from their sleeping silks and furs upon the deck near by.

The cruiser-transport lay without lights, and, resting as she was upon the ground, must have been entirely invisible to the oncoming flier, which all presently recognized as a small craft.

It soon became evident that the stranger intended making a landing, for she was now spiraling slowly above them, dropping lower and lower in each graceful curve.

"It is the *Thuria*," whispered one of the Dusarian warriors. "I would know her in the blackness of the pits among ten thousand other craft."

"Right you are!" exclaimed Vas Kor, who had come on deck. And then he hailed:

"Kaor, *Thuria!*"

"Kaor!" came presently from above after a brief silence. Then: "What ship?"

"Cruiser-transport *Kalksus*, Vas Kor of Dusar."

"Good!" came from above. "Is there safe landing alongside?"

"Yes, close in to starboard. Wait, we will show our lights," and a moment later the smaller craft settled close beside the *Kalksus*, and the lights of the latter were immediately extinguished once more.

Several figures could be seen slipping over the side of the *Thuria* and advancing toward the *Kalksus*. Ever suspicious, the Dusarians stood ready to receive the visitors as friends or foes as closer inspection might prove them.

Carthoris stood quite near the rail, ready to take sides with the new-comers should chance have it that they were Heliumites playing a bold stroke of strategy upon this lone Dusarian ship. He had led like parties himself, and knew that such a contingency was quite possible.

But the face of the first man to cross the rail undeceived him with a shock that was not at all unpleasurable—it was the face of Astok, Prince of Dusar.

Scarce noticing the others upon the deck of the *Kalksus*, Astok strode forward to accept Vas Kor's greeting, then he summoned the noble below. The warriors and officers returned to their sleeping silks and furs, and once more the deck was deserted except for the Dusarian warrior and Turjun, the panthan, who stood guard.

The latter walked quietly to and fro. The former leaned across the rail, wishing for the hour that would bring him relief. He did not see his companion approach the lights of the cabin of Vas Kor. He did not see him stoop with ear close pressed to a tiny ventilator.

"May the white apes take us all," cried Astok ruefully, "if we are not in as ugly a snarl as you have ever seen! Nutus thinks that we have her in hiding far away from Dusar. He has bidden me bring her here."

He paused. No man should have heard from his lips the thing he was trying to tell. It should have been for ever the secret of Nutus and Astok, for upon it rested the safety of a throne. With that knowledge any man could wrest from the Jeddak of Dusar whatever he listed.

But Astok was afraid, and he wanted from this older man the suggestion of an alternative. He went on.

"I am to kill her," he whispered, looking fearfully around. "Nutus merely wishes to see the body that he may know his commands have been executed. I am now suppposed to be gone to the spot where we have her hidden that I may fetch her in secrecy to Dusar. None is to know that she has ever been in the keeping of a Dusarian. I do not need to tell you what would befal Dusar should Ptarth and Helium and Kaol ever learn the truth."

The jaws of the listener at the ventilator clicked together with a vicious snap. Before he had but guessed at the identity of the subject of this conversation. Now he knew. And they were to kill her! His muscular fingers clenched until the nails bit into the palms.

"And you wish me to go with you while you fetch her to Dusar," Vas Kor was saying. "Where is she?"

Astok bent close and whispered into the other's ear. The suggestion of a smile crossed the cruel features of Vas Kor. He realized the power that lay within his grasp. He should be a jed at least.

"And how may I help you, my Prince?" asked the older man suavely.

"I cannot kill her," said Astok. "Issus! I cannot do it! When she turns those eyes upon me my heart becomes water."

Vas Kor's eyes narrowed.

"And you wish——" He paused, the interrogation unfinished, yet complete.

Astok nodded.

"*You* do not love her," he said.

"But I love my life—though I am only a lesser noble," he concluded meaningly.

"You shall be a greater noble—a noble of the first rank!" exclaimed Astok.

"I would be a jed," said Vas Kor bluntly.

Astok hesitated.

"A jed must die before there can be another jed," he pleaded.

"Jeds have died before," snapped Vas Kor. "It would doubtless be not difficult for you to find a jed you do not love, Astok—there are many who do not love you."

Already Vas Kor was commencing to presume upon his power over the young prince. Astok was quick to note and appreciate the subtle change in his lieutenant. A cunning scheme entered his weak and wicked brain.

"As you say, Vas Kor!" he exclaimed. "You shall be a jed when the thing is done," and then, to himself: "Nor will it then be difficult for me to find a jed I do not love."

"When shall we return to Dusar?" asked the noble.

"At once," replied Astok. "Let us get under way now—there is naught to keep you here?"

"I had intended sailing on the morrow, picking up such recruits as the various Dwars of the Roads might have collected for me, as we returned to Dusar."

"Let the recruits wait," said Astok. "Or, better still, come you to Dusar upon the *Thuria,* leaving the *Kalksus* to follow and pick up the recruits."

"Yes," acquiesced Vas Kor; "that is the better plan. Come; I am ready," and he rose to accompany Astok to the latter's flier.

The listener at the ventilator came to his feet slowly, like an old man. His face was drawn and pinched and very white beneath the light copper of his skin. She was to die! And he helpless to avert the tragedy. He did not even know where she was imprisoned.

The two men were ascending from the cabin to the deck. Turjun, the pantha, crept close to the companion-way, his sinuous fingers closing tightly upon the hilt of his dagger. Could he despatch them both before he was over-powered? He smiled. He could slay an entire utan of her enemies in his present state of mind.

They were almost abreast of him now. Astok was speaking.

"Bring a couple of your men along, Vas Kor," he said. "We are short-handed upon the *Thuria,* so quickly did we depart."

The panthan's fingers dropped from the dagger's hilt. His quick mind had grasped here a chance for succouring Thuvia of Ptarth. He might be chosen as one to accompany the assassins, and once he had learned where the captive lay he could despatch Astok and Vas Kor as well as now. To kill them before he knew where Thuvia was hid was simply to leave her to death at the hands of others; for sooner or later Nutus would learn her whereabouts, and Nutus, Jeddak of Dusar, could not afford to let her live.

Turjun put himself in the path of Vas Kor that he

might not be overlooked. The noble aroused the men sleeping upon the deck, but always before him the strange panthan whom he had recruited that same day found means for keeping himself to the fore.

Vas Kor turned to his lieutenant, giving instruction for the bringing of the *Kalksus* to Dusar, and the gathering up of the recruits; then he signed to two warriors who stood close behind the padwar.

"You two accompany us to the *Thuria,*" he said, "and put yourselves at the disposal of her dwar."

It was dark upon the deck of the *Kalksus,* so Vas Kor had not a good look at the faces of the two he chose; but that was of no moment, for they were but common warriors to assist with the ordinary duties upon a flier, and to fight if need be.

One of the two was Kar Komak, the bowman. The other was not Carthoris.

The Heliumite was mad with disappointment. He snatched his dagger from his harness; but already Astok had left the deck of the *Kalksus,* and he knew that before he could overtake him, should he dispatch Vas Kor, he would be killed by the Dusarian warriors, who now were thick upon the deck. With either one of the two alive Thuvia was in as great danger as though both lived—it must be both!

As Vas Kor descended to the ground Carthoris boldly followed him, nor did any attempt to halt him, thinking, doubtless, that he was one of the party.

After him came Kar Komak and the Dusarian warrior who had been detailed to duty upon the *Thuria*. Carthoris walked close to the left side of the latter. Now they came to the dense shadow under the side of the *Thuria*. It was very dark there, so that they had to grope for the ladder.

Kar Komak preceded the Dusarian. The latter reached upward for the swinging rounds, and as he did so steel fingers closed upon his windpipe and a steel blade pierced the very centre of his heart.

Turjun, the panthan, was the last to clamber over the

rail of the *Thuria,* drawing the rope ladder in after him.

A moment later the flier was rising rapidly, headed for the north.

At the rail Kar Komak turned to speak to the warrior who had been detailed to accompany him. His eyes went wide as they rested upon the face of the young man whom he had met beside the granite cliffs that guard mysterious Lothar. How had he come in place of the Dusarian?

A quick sign, and Kar Komak turned once more to find the *Thuria's* dwar that he might report himself for duty. Behind him followed the panthan.

Carthoris blessed the chance that had caused Vas Kor to choose the bowman of all others, for had it been another Dusarian there would have been questions to answer as to the whereabouts of the warrior who lay so quietly in the field beyond the residence of Hal Vas, Dwar of the Southern Road; and Carthoris had no answer to that question other than his sword point, which alone was scarce adequate to convince the entire crew of the *Thuria.*

The journey to Dusar seemed interminable to the impatient Carthoris, though as a matter of fact it was quickly accomplished. Some time before they reached their destination they met and spoke with another Dusarian war flier. From it they learned that a great battle was soon to be fought south-east of Dusar.

The combined navies of Dusar, Ptarth and Kaol had been intercepted in their advance toward Helium by the mighty Heliumitic navy—the most formidable upon Barsoom, not alone in numbers and armament, but in the training and courage of its officers and warriors, and the zitidaric proportions of many of its monster battleships.

Not for many a day had there been the promise of such a battle. Four jeddaks were in direct command of their own fleets—Kulan Tith of Kaol, Thuvan Dihn of Ptarth, and Nutus of Duaar upon one side; while upon the other was Tardos Mors, Jeddak of Helium. With the latter was John Carter, Warlord of Mars.

From the far north another force was moving south across the barrier cliffs—the new navy of Talu, Jeddak of Okar, coming in response to the call from the warlord. Upon the decks of the sullen ships of war black-bearded yellow men looked over eagerly toward the south. Gorgeous were they in their splendid cloaks of orluk and apt. Fierce, formidable fighters from the hothouse cities of the frozen north.

And from the distant south, from the sea of Omean and the cliffs of gold, from the temples of the therns and the gardens of Issus, other thousands sailed into the north at the call of the great man they all had learned to respect, and, respecting, love. Pacing the flagship of this mighty fleet, second only to the navy of Helium, was the ebon godar, Jeddak of the First Born, his heart beating strong in anticipation of the coming moment when he should hurl his savage crews and the weight of his mighty ships upon the enemies of the warlord.

But would these allies reach the theatre of war in time to be of avail to Helium? Or, would Helium need them?

Carthoris, with the other members of the crew of the *Thuria*, heard the gossip and the rumours. None knew of the two fleets, the one from the south and the other from the north, that were coming to support the ships of Helium, and all of Dusar were convinced that nothing now could save the ancient power of Helium from being wiped for ever from the upper air of Barsoom.

Carthoris, too, loyal son of Helium that he was, felt that even his beloved navy might not be able to cope successfully with the combined forces of three great powers.

Now the *Thuria* touched the landing-stage above the palace of Astok. Hurriedly the prince and Vas Kor disembarked and entered the drop that would carry them to the lower levels of the palace.

Close beside it was another drop that was utilized by common warriors. Carthoris touched Kar Komak upon the arm.

"Come!" he whispered. "You are my only friend among a nation of enemies. Will you stand by me?"

"To the death," replied Kar Komak.

The two approached the drop. A slave operated it.

"Where are your passes?" he asked.

Carthoris fumbled in his pocket pouch as though in search of them, at the same time entering the cage. Kar Komak followed him, closing the door. The slave did not start the cage downward. Every second counted. They must reach the lower level as soon as possible after Astok and Vas Kor if they would know whither the two went.

Carthoris turned suddenly upon the slave, hurling him to the opposite side of the cage.

"Bind and gag him, Kar Komak!" he cried.

Then he grasped the control lever, and as the cage shot downward at sickening speed, the bowman grappled with the slave. Carthoris could not leave the control to assist his companion, for should they touch the lowest level at the speed at which they were going, all would be dashed to instant death.

Below him he could now see the top of Astok's cage in the parallel shaft, and he reduced the speed of his to that of the other. The slave commenced to scream.

"Silence him!" cried Carthoris.

A moment later a limp form crumpled to the floor of the cage.

"He is silenced," said Kar Komak.

Carthoris brought the cage to a sudden stop at one of the higher levels of the palace. Opening the door, he grasped the still form of the slave and pushed it out upon the floor. Then he banged the gate and resumed the downward drop.

Once more he sighted the top of the cage that held Astok and Vas Kor. An instant later it had stopped, and as he brought his car to a halt, he saw the two men disappear through one of the exits of the corridor beyond.

CHAPTER XIV

KULAN TITH'S SACRIFICE

THE MORNING of the second day of her incarceration in the east tower of the palace of Astok, Prince of Dusar, found Thuvia of Ptarth waiting in dull apathy the coming of the assassin.

She had exhausted every possibility of escape, going over and over again the door and the windows, the floor and the walls.

The solid ersite slabs she could not even scratch; the tough Barsoomian glass of the windows would have shattered to nothing less than a heavy sledge in the hands of a strong man. The door and the lock were impregnable. There was no escape. And they had stripped her of her weapons so that she could not even anticipate the hour of her doom, thus robbing them of the satisfaction of witnessing her last moments.

When would they come? Would Astok do the deed with his own hands? She doubted that he had the courage for it. At heart he was a coward—she had known it since first she had heard him brag as, a visitor at the court of her father, he had sought to impress her with his valour.

She could not help but compare him with another. And with whom would an affianced bride compare an unsuccessful suitor? With her betrothed? And did Thuvia of Ptarth now measure Astok of Dusar by the standards of Kulan Tith, Jeddak of Kaol?

She was about to die; her thoughts were her own to do with as she pleased; yet furthest from them was Kulan Tith. Instead the figure of the tall and comely Heliumite filled her mind, crowding therefrom all other images.

She dreamed of his noble face, the quiet dignity of his bearing, the smile that lit his eyes as he conversed with his friends, and the smile that touched his lips as he fought with his enemies—the fighting smile of his Virginian sire.

And Thuvia of Ptarth, true daughter of Barsoom, found her breath quickening and heart leaping to the memory of this other smile—the smile that she would never see again. With a little half-sob the girl sank to the pile of silks and furs that were tumbled in confusion beneath the east window, burying her face in her arms.

In the corridor outside her prison-room two men had paused in heated argument.

"I tell you again, Astok," one was saying, "that I shall not do this thing unless you be present in the room."

There was little of the respect due royalty in the tone of the speaker's voice. The other, noting it, flushed.

"Do not impose too far upon my friendship for you, Vas Kor," he snapped. "There is a limit to my patience."

"There is no question of royal prerogative here," returned Vas Kor. "You ask me to become an assassin in your stead, and against your jeddak's strict injunctions. You are in no position, Astok, to dictate to me; but rather should you be glad to accede to my reasonable request that you be present, thus sharing the guilt with me. Why should I bear it all?"

The younger man scowled, but he advanced toward the locked door, and as it swung in upon its hinges, he entered the room beyond at the side of Vas Kor.

Across the chamber the girl, hearing them enter, rose to her feet and faced them. Under the soft copper of her skin she blanched just a trifle; but her eyes were brave and level, and the haughty tilt of her firm little chin was eloquent of loathing and contempt.

"You still prefer death?" asked Astok.

"To *you*, yes," replied the girl coldly.

The Prince of Dusar turned to Vas Kor and nodded. The noble drew his short-sword and crossed the room toward Thuvia.

"Kneel!" he commanded.

"I prefer to die standing," she replied.

"As you will," said Vas Kor, feeling the point of his blade with his left thumb. "In the name of Nutus, Jeddak of Dusar!" he cried, and ran quickly toward her.

"In the name of Carthoris, Prince of Helium!" came in low tones from the doorway.

Vas Kor turned to see the panthan he had recruited at his son's house leaping across the floor toward him. The fellow brushed past Astok with an: "After him, you —calot!"

Vas Kor wheeled to meet the charging man.

"What means this treason?" he cried.

Astok, with bared sword, leaped to Vas Kor's assistance. The panthan's sword clashed against that of the noble, and in the first encounter Vas Kor knew that he faced a master swordsman.

Before he half realized the stranger's purpose he found the man between himself and Thuvia of Ptarth, at bay facing the two swords of the Dusarians. But he fought not like a man at bay. Ever was he the aggressor, and though always he kept his flashing blade between the girl and her enemies, yet he managed to force them hither and thither about the room, calling to the girl to follow close behind him.

Until it was too late neither Vas Kor nor Astok dreamed of that which lay in the panthan's mind; but at last as the fellow stood with his back toward the door, both understood—they were penned in their own prison, and now the intruder could slay them at his will, for Thuvia of Ptarth was bolting the door at the man's direction, first taking the key from the opposite side, where Astok had left it when they had entered.

Astok, as was his way, finding that the enemy did not fall immediately before their swords, was leaving the brunt of the fighting to Vas Kor, and now as his eyes appraised the panthan carefully they presently went wider and wider, for slowly he had come to recognize the features of the Prince of Helium.

The Heliumite was pressing close upon Vas Kor. The noble was bleeding from a dozen wounds. Astok saw that he could not for long withstand the cunning craft of that terrible sword hand.

"Courage, Vas Kor!" he whispered in the other's ear. "I have a plan. Hold him but a moment longer and all will be well," but the balance of the sentence, "with Astok, Prince of Dusar," he did not voice aloud.

Vas Kor, dreaming no treachery, nodded his head, and for a moment succeeded in holding Carthoris at bay. Then the Heliumite and the girl saw the Dusarian prince run swiftly to the opposite side of the chamber, touch something in the wall that sent a great panel swinging inward, and disappear into the black vault beyond.

It was done so quickly that by no possibility could they have intercepted him. Carthoris, fearful lest Vas Kor might similarly elude him, or Astok return immediately with reinforcements, sprang viciously in upon his antagonist, and a moment later the headless body of the Dusarian noble rolled upon the ersite floor.

"Come!" cried Carthoris. "There is no time to be lost. Astok will be back in a moment with enough warriors to overpower me."

But Astok had no such plan in mind, for such a move would have meant the spreading of the fact among the palace gossips that the Ptarthian princess was a prisoner in the east tower. Quickly would the word have come to his father, and no amount of falsifying could have explained away the facts that the jeddak's investigation would have brought to light.

Instead Astok was racing madly through a long corridor to reach the door of the tower-room before Carthoris and Thuvia left the apartment. He had seen the girl remove the key and place it in her pocket-pouch, and he knew that a dagger point driven into the keyhole from the opposite side would imprison them in the secret chamber till eight dead worlds circled a cold, dead sun.

As fast as he could run Astok entered the main corridor that led to the tower chamber. Would he reach the door in time? What if the Heliumite should have already emerged and he should run upon him in the passageway? Astok felt a cold chill run up his spine. He had no stomach to face that uncanny blade.

He was almost at the door. Around the next turn of the corridor it stood. No, they had not left the apartment. Evidently Vas Kor was still holding the Heliumite!

Astok could scarce repress a grin at the clever manner in which he had outwitted the noble and disposed of him at the same time. And then he rounded the turn and came face to face with an auburn-haired, white giant.

The fellow did not wait to ask the reason for his coming; instead he leaped upon him with a long-sword, so that Astok had to parry a dozen vicious cuts before he could disengage himself and flee back down the runway.

A moment later Carthoris and Thuvia entered the corridor from the secret chamber.

"Well, Kar Komak?" asked the Heliumite.

"It is fortunate that you left me here, red man," said the bowman. "I but just now intercepted one who seemed over-anxious to reach this door—it was he whom they call Astok, Prince of Dusar."

Carthoris smiled.

"Where is he now?" he asked.

"He escaped my blade, and ran down this corridor," replied Kar Komak.

"We must lose no time, then!" exclaimed Carthoris. "He will have the guard upon us yet!"

Together the three hastened along the winding passages through which Carthoris and Kar Komak had tracked the Dusarians by the marks of the latter's sandals in the thin dust that overspread the floors of these seldom-used passage-ways.

They had come to the chamber at the entrances to the

lifts before they met with opposition. Here they found a handful of guardsmen, and an officer, who, seeing that they were strangers, questioned their presence in the palace of Astok.

Once more Cathoris and Kar Komak had recourse to their blades, and before they had won their way to one of the lifts the noise of the conflict must have aroused the entire palace, for they heard men shouting, and as they passed the many levels on their quick passage to the landing-stage they saw armed men running hither and thither in search of the cause of the commotion.

Beside the stage lay the *Thuria,* with three warriors on guard. Again the Heliumite and the Lotharian fought shoulder to shoulder, but the battle was soon over, for the Prince of Helium alone would have been a match for any three that Dusar could produce.

Scarce had the *Thuria* risen from the ways ere a hundred or more fighting men leaped to view upon the landing-stage. At their head was Astok of Dusar, and as he saw the two he had thought so safely in his power slipping from his grasp, he danced with rage and chagrin, shaking his fists and hurling abuse and vile insults at them.

With her bow inclined upward at a dizzy angle, the *Thuria* shot meteor-like into the sky. From a dozen points swift patrol boats darted after her, for the scene upon the landing-stage above the palace of the Prince of Dusar had not gone unnoticed.

A dozen times shots grazed the *Thuria's* side, and as Carthoris could not leave the control levers, Thuvia of Ptarth turned the muzzles of the craft's rapid-fire guns upon the enemy as she clung to the steep and slippery surface of the deck.

It was a noble race and a noble fight. One against a score now, for other Dusarian craft had joined in the pursuit; but Astok, Prince of Dusar, had built well when he built the *Thuria.* None in the navy of his sire possessed a swifter flier; no other craft so well armoured or so well armed.

One by one the pursuers were distanced, and as the

last of them fell out of range behind, Carthoris dropped the *Thuria's* nose to a horizontal plane, as with lever drawn to the last notch, she tore through the thin air of dying Mars toward the east and Ptarth.

Thirteen and a half thousand haads away lay Ptarth —a stiff thirty-hour journey for the swiftest of fliers, and between Dusar and Ptarth might lie half the navy of Dusar, for in this direction was the reported seat of the great naval battle that even now might be in progress.

Could Carthoris have known precisely where the great fleets of the contending nations lay, he would have hastened to them without delay, for in the return of Thuvia to her sire lay the greatest hope of peace.

Half the distance they covered without sighting a single warship, and then Kar Komak called Carthoris's attention to a distant craft that rested upon the ochre vegetation of the great dead seabottom, above which the *Thuria* was speeding.

About the vessel many figures could be seen swarming. With the aid of powerful glasses, the Heliumite saw that they were green warriors, and that they were repeatedly charging down upon the crew of the stranded airship. The nationality of the latter he could not make out at so great a distance.

It was not necessary to change the course of the *Thuria* to permit of passing directly above the scene of battle, but Carthoris dropped his craft a few hundred feet that he might have a better and closer view.

If the ship was of a friendly power, he could do no less than stop and direct his guns upon her enemies, though with the precious freight he carried he scarcely felt justified in landing, for he could offer but two swords in reinforcement—scarce enough to warrant jeopardizing the safety of the Princess of Ptarth.

As they came close above the stricken ship, they could see that it would be but a question of minutes before the green horde would swarm across the armoured bulwarks to glut the ferocity of their bloodlust upon the defenders.

"It would be futile to descend," said Carthoris to

Thuvia. "The craft may even be of Dusar—she shows no insignia. All that we may do is fire upon the hordesman"; and as he spoke he stepped to one of the guns and deflected its muzzle toward the green warriors at the ship's side.

At the first shot from the *Thuria* those upon the vessel below evidently discovered her for the first time. Immediately a device fluttered from the bow of the warship on the ground. Thuvia of Ptarth caught her breath quickly, glancing at Carthoris.

The device was that of Kulan Tith, Jeddak of Kaol— the man to whom the Princess of Ptarth was betrothed!

How easy for the Heliumite to pass on, leaving his rival to the fate that could not for long be averted! No man could accuse him of cowardice or treachery, for Kulan Tith was in arms against Helium, and, further, upon the *Thuria* were not enough swords to delay even temporarily the outcome that already was a foregone conclusion in the minds of the watchers.

What would Carthoris, Prince of Helium, do?

Scarce had the device broken to the faint breeze ere the bow of the *Thuria* dropped at a sharp angle toward the ground.

"Can you navigate her?" asked Carthoris of Thuvia. The girl nodded.

"I am going to try to take the survivors aboard," he continued. "It will need both Kar Komak and myself to man the guns while the Kaolians take to the boarding tackle. Keep her bow depressed against the rifle fire. She can bear it better in her forward armour, and at the same time the propellers will be protected."

He hurried to the cabin as Thuvia took the control. A moment later the boarding tackle dropped from the keel of the *Thuria,* and from a dozen points along either side stout, knotted leathern lines trailed downward. At the same time a signal broke from her bow:

"Prepare to board us."

A shout arose from the deck of the Kaolian warship. Carthoris, who by this time had returned from the cabin, smiled sadly. He was about to snatch from the jaws of death the man who stood between himself and the woman he loved.

"Take the port bow gun, Kar Komak," he called to the bowman, and himself stepped to the gun upon the starboard bow.

They could now feel the sharp shock of the explosions of the green warriors vomited their hail of death and desides of the staunch *Thuria.*

It was a forlorn hope at best. At any moment the repulsive ray tanks might be pierced. The men upon the Kaolian ship were battling with renewed hope. In the bow stood Kulan Tith, a brave figure fighting beside his brave warriors, beating back the ferocious green men.

The *Thuria* came low above the other craft. The Kaolians were forming under their officers in readiness to board, and then a sudden fierce fusillade from the rifles of the green arriors vomited their hail of death and destruction into the side of the brave flier.

Like a wounded bird she dived suddenly Marsward careening drunkenly. Thuvia turned the bow upward in an effort to avert the imminent tragedy, but she succeeded only in lessening the shock of the flier's impact as she struck the ground beside the Kaolian ship.

When the green men saw only two warriors and a woman upon the deck of the *Thuria,* a savage shout of triumph arose from their ranks, while an answering groan broke from the lips of the Kaolians.

The former now turned their attention upon the new arrival, for they saw her defenders could soon be overcome and that from her deck they could command the deck of the better-manned ship.

As they charged a shout of warning came from Kulan Tith, upon the bridge of his own ship, and with it an appreciation of the valour of the act that had put the smaller vessel in these sore straits.

"Who is it," he cried, "that offers his life in the service of Kulan Tith? Never was wrought a nobler deed of self-sacrifice upon Barsoom!"

The green horde was scrambling over the *Thuria's* side as there broke from the bow the device of Carthoris, Prince of Helium, in reply to the query of the jeddak of Kaol. None upon the smaller flier had opportunity to note the effect of this announcement upon the Kaolians, for their attention was claimed solely now by that which was transpiring upon their own deck.

Kar Komak stood behind the gun he had been operating, staring with wide eyes at the onrushing hideous green warriors. Carthoris, seeing him thus, felt a pang of regret that, after all, this man that he had thought so valorous should prove, in the hour of need, as spineless as Jav or Tario.

"Kar Komak—the man!" he shouted. "Grip yourself! Remember the days of the glory of the seafarers of Lothar. Fight! Fight, man! Fight as never man fought before. All that remains to us is to die fighting."

Kar Komak turned toward the Heliumite, a grim smile upon his lips.

"Why should we fight," he asked. "Against such fearful odds? There is another way—a better way. Look!" He pointed toward the companion-way that led below deck.

The green men, a handful of them, had already reached the *Thuria's* deck, as Carthoris glanced in the direction the Lotharian had indicated. The sight that met his eyes set his heart to thumping in joy and relief —Thuvia of Ptarth might yet be saved? For from below there poured a stream of giant bowmen, grim and terrible. Not the bowmen of Tario or Jav, but the bowmen of an odwar of bowmen—savage fighting men, eager for the fray.

The green warriors paused in momentary surprise and consternation, but only for a moment. Then with horrid war-cries they leaped forward to meet these strange, new foemen.

A volley of arrows stopped them in their tracks. In a moment the only green warriors upon the deck of the *Thuria* were dead warriors, and the bowmen of Kar

Komak were leaping over the vessel's sides to charge the hordesmen upon the ground.

Utan after utan tumbled from the bowels of the *Thuria* to launch themselves upon the unfortunate green men. Kulan Tith and his Kaolians stood wide-eyed and speechless with amazement as they saw thousands of these strange, fierce warriors emerge from the companion-way of the small craft that could not comfortably have accommodated more than fifty.

At last the green men could withstand the onslaught of overwhelming numbers no longer. Slowly, at first, they fell back across the ochre plain. The bowmen pursued them. Kar Komak, standing upon the deck of the *Thuria,* trembled with excitement.

At the top of his lungs he voiced the savage war-cry of his forgotten day. He roared encouragement and commands at his battling utans, and then, as they charged further and further from the *Thuria,* he could no longer withstand the lure of battle.

Leaping over the ship's side to the ground, he joined the last of his bowmen as they raced off over the dead sea-bottom in pursuit of the fleeing green horde.

Beyond a low promontory of what once had been an island the green men were disappearing toward the west. Close upon their heels raced the fleet bowmen of a by-gone day, and forging steadily ahead among them Carthoris and Thuvia could see the mighty figure of Kar Komak, brandishing aloft the Torquasian short-sword with which he was armed, as he urged his creatures after the retreating enemy.

As the last of them disappeared behind the promontory, Carthoris turned toward Thuvia of Ptarth.

"They have taught me a lesson, these vanishing bowmen of Lothar," he said. "When they have served their purpose they remain not to embarrass their masters by their presence. Kulan Tith and his warriors are here to protect you. My acts have constituted the proof of my honesty of purpose. Good-bye," and he knelt at her feet, raising a bit of her harness to his lips.

The girl reached out a hand and laid it upon the thick black hair of the head bent before her. Softly she asked:

"Where are you going, Carthoris?"

"With Kar Komak, the bowman," he replied. "There will be fighting and forgetfulness."

The girl put her hands before her eyes, as though to shut out some mighty temptation from her sight.

"May my ancestors have mercy upon me," she cried, "if I say the thing I have no right to say; but I cannot see you cast your life away, Carthoris, Prince of Helium! Stay, my chieftain. Stay—I love you!"

A cough behind them brought both about, and there they saw standing, not two paces from them Kulan Tith, Jeddak of Kaol.

For a long moment none spoke. Then Kluan Tith cleared his throat.

"I could not help hearing all that passed," he said. "I am no fool, to be blind to the love that lies between you. Nor am I blind to the lofty honour that has caused you, Carthoris, to risk your life and hers to save mine, though you thought that that very act would rob you of the chance to keep her for your own.

"Nor can I fail to appreciate the virtue that has kept your lips sealed against words of love for this Heliumite, Thuvia, for I know that I have but just heard the first declaration of your passion for him. I do not condemn you. Rather should I have condemned you had you entered a loveless marriage with me.

"Take back your liberty, Thuvia of Ptarth," he cried, "and bestow it where your heart already lies enchained, and when the golden collars are clasped about your necks you will see that Kulan Tith's is the first sword to be raised in declaration of eternal friendship for the new Princess of Helium and her royal mate!"

A GLOSSARY OF NAMES AND TERMS USED
IN THE MARTIN BOOKS

Aaanthor. A dead city of ancient Mars.

Aisle of Hope. An aisle leading to the court-room in Helium.

Apt. An Arctic monster. A huge, white-furred creature with six limbs, four of which, short and heavy, carry it over the snow and ice; the other two, which grow forward from its shoulders on either side of its long, powerful neck, terminate in white, hairless hands with which it seizes and holds its prey. Its head and mouth are similar in appearance to those of a hippopotamus, except that from the sides of the lower jawbone two mighty horns curve slightly downward toward the front. Its two huge eyes extend in two vast oval patches from the centre of the top of the cranium down either side of the head to below the roots of the horns, so that these weapons really grow out from the lower part of the eyes, which are composed of several thousand ocelli each. Each ocellus is furnished with its own lid, and the apt can, at will, close as many of the facets of his huge eyes as he chooses. (See THE WARLORD OF MARS.)

Astok. Prince of Dusar.

Avenue of Ancestors. A street in Helium.

Banth. Barsoomian lion. A fierce beast of prey that roams the low hills surrounding the dead seas of ancient Mars. It is almost hairless, having only a great, bristly mane about its thick neck. Its long, lithe body is supported by ten powerful legs, its enormous jaws are equipped

153

with several rows of long needle-like fangs, and its mouth reaches to a point far back of its tiny ears. It has enormous protruding eyes of green. (See THE GODS OF MARS.)

Bar Comas. Jeddak of Warhoon. (See A PRINCESS OF MARS.)

Barsoom. MARS.

Black pirates of Barsoom. Men six feet and over in height. Have clear-cut and handsome features; their eyes are well set and large, though a slight narrowness lends them a crafty appearance. The iris is extremely black while the eyeball itself is quite white and clear. Their skin has the appearance of polished ebony. (See THE GODS OF MARS.)

Calot. A dog. About the size of a Shetland pony and has ten short legs. The head bears a slight resemblance to that of a frog, except that the jaws are equipped with three rows of long, sharp tusks. (See A PRINCESS OF MARS.)

Carter, John. Warlord of Mars.

Carthoris of Helium. Son of John Carter and Dejah Thoris.

Dak Kova. Jed among the Warhoons (later jeddak).

Darseen. Chameleon-like reptile.

Dator. Chief or prince among the First Born.

Dejah Thoris. Princess of Helium.

Djor Kantos. Son of Kantos Kan; padwar of the Fifth Utan.

Dor. Valley of Heaven.

Dotar Sojat. John Carter's Martian name, from the surnames of the first two warrior chieftains he killed.

Dusar. A Martian kingdom.

Dwar. Captain.

Ersite. A kind of stone.

Father of Therns. High Priest of religious cult.

First Born. Black race; black pirates.

Kar Komak. Odwar of Lotharian bowmen.

Gate of Jeddaks. A gate in Helium.

Gozava. Tars Tarkas' dead wife.

Gur Tus. Dwar of the Tenth Utan.

Haad. Martian mile.

Hal Vas. Son of Vas Kor the Dusarian noble.

Hastor. A city of Helium.

Hekkador. Title of Father of Therns.

Helium. The empire of the grandfather of Dejah Thoris.

Holy Therns. A Martian religious cult.

Hortan Gur. Jeddak of Torquas.

Hor Vastus. Padwar in the navy of Helium.

Horz. Deserted city; Barsoomian Greenwich.

Illall. A city of Okar.

Iss. River of Death. (See A PRINCESS OF MARS.)

Issus. Goddess of Death, whose abode is upon the banks of the Lost Sea of Korus. (See THE GODS OF MARS.)

Jav. A Lotharian.

Jed. King.

Jeddak. Emperor.

Kab Kadja. Jeddak of the Warhoons of the south.

Kadabra. Capital of Okar.

Kadar. Guard.

Kalkans. Cruiser; transport under Vas Kor.

Kantos Kan. Padwar in the Helium navy.

Koal. A Martian kingdom in the eastern hemisphere.

Kaor. Greeting.

Karad. Martian degree.

Komal. The Lotharian god; a huge banth.

Korad. A dead city of ancient Mars. (See A PRINCESS OF MARS.)

Korus. The Lost Sea of Dor.

Kulan Tith. Jeddak of Kaol. (See THE WARLORD OF MARS.)

Lakor. A thern.

Larok. A Dusarian warrior; artificer.

Lorquas Ptomel. Jed among the Tharks. (See A PRINCESS OF MARS.)

Lothar. The forgotten city.

Marentina. A principality of Okar.

Matai Shang. Father of Therns. (See THE GODS OF MARS.)

Mors Kajak. A jed of lesser Helium.

Notan. Royal psychologist of Zodanga.

Nutus. Jeddak of Dusar.

Od. Martian foot.

Odwar. A commander, or general.

Okar. Land of the yellow men.

Old Ben (or *Uncle Ben*). The writer's body-servant (coloured).

Omad. Man with one name.

Omean. The buried sea.

Orluk. A black and yellow striped Arctic monster.

Otz Mountains. Surrounding the alley Dor and the Lost Sea of Korus.

Padwar. Lieutenant.

Panthan. A soldier of fortune.

Parthak. The Zodangan who brought food to John Carter in the pits of Zat Arras. (See THE GODS OF MARS.)

Pedestal of Truth. Within the courtroom of Helium.

Phaidor. Daughter of Matai Shang. (See THE GODS OF MARS.)

Pimalia. Gorgeous flowering plant.

Plant men of Barsoom. A race inhabiting the Valley Dor. They are ten or twelve feet in height when standing erect; their arms are very short and fashioned after the manner of an elephant's trunk, being sinuous; the body is hairless and ghoulish blue except for a broad band of white which encircles the protruding, single eye, the pupil, iris and ball of which are dead white. The nose is a ragged, inflamed, circular hole in the centre of the blank face, resembling a fresh bullet wound which has not yet commenced to bleed. There is no mouth in the head. With the exception of the face, the head is covered by a tangled mass of jet-black hair some eight or ten inches in length. Each hair is about the thickness of a large angleworm. The body, legs and feet are of human shape but of monstrous proportions, the feet being fully three feet long and very flat and broad. The method of feeding consists in running their odd hands over the surface of the turf, cropping off the tender vegetation with razor-like talons and sucking it up from two mouths, which lie one in the palm of each hand. They are equipped with a massive tail about six feet long, quite round where it joins the body, but tapering to a flat, thin blade toward the end, which trails at right angles to the ground. (See THE GODS OF MARS.)

Prince Soran. Overlord of the navy of Ptarth.

Ptarth. A Martian kingdom.

Ptor. Family name of three Zodangan brothers.

Sab Than. Prince of Zodanga. (See A PRINCESS OF MARS.)

Safad. A Martian inch.

Sak. Jump.

Salensus Oll. Jeddak of Okar. (See THE WARLORD OF MARS.)

Saran Tal. Carthoris' major-domo.

Sarkoja. A green Martian woman. (See A PRINCESS OF MARS.)

Sator Throg. A Holy Thern of the Tenth Cycle.

Shador. Island in Omean used as a prison.

Silian. Slimy reptiles inhabiting the Sea of Korus.

Sith. Hornet-like monster. Bald-faced and about the size of a Hereford bull. Has frightful jaws in front and mighty poisoned sting behind. The eyes, of myriad facets, cover three-fourths of the head, permitting the creature to see in all directions at one and the same time. (See THE WARLORD OF MARS.)

Skeel. A Martian hardwood.

Sola. A young green Martian woman.

Solan. An official of the palace.

Sompus. A kind of tree.

Sorak. A little pet animal among the red Martian women, about the size of a cat.

Sorapus. A Martian hardwood.

Sorav. An officer of Salensus Oll.

Tal. A Martian second.

Tal Hajus. Jeddak of Thark.

Talu. Rebel Prince of Marentina.

Tan Gama. Warhoon warrior.

Tardos Mors. Grandfather of Dejah Thoris and Jeddak of Helium.

Tario. Jeddak of Lothar.

Tars Tarkas. A green man, chieftain of the Tharks.

Temple of Reward. In Helium.

Tenth Cycle. A sphere, or plane of eminence, among the Holy Therns.

Thabis. Issus' chief.

Than Kosis. Jeddak of Zodanga. (See A PRINCESS OF MARS.)

Thark. City and name of a green Martian horde.

Thoat. A green Martian horse. Ten feet high at the shoulder, with four legs on either side; a broad, flat tail, larger at the tip than at the root which it holds straight out behind while running; a mouth splitting its head from snout to the long, massive neck. It is entirely devoid of hair and is of a dark slate colour and exceedingly smooth and glossy. It has a white belly and the legs are shaded from slate at the shoulders and hips to a vivid yellow at the feet. The feet are heavily padded and nailless. (See A PRINCESS OF MARS.)

Thor-Ban. Jed among the green men of Torquas.

Thorian. Chief of the lesser Therns.

Throne of Righteousness. In the court-room of Helium.

Throxus. Mightiest of the five oceans.

Thurds. A green horde inimical to Torquas.

Thuria. The nearer moon.

Thurid. A black dator.

Thuvan Dihn. Jeddak of Ptarth.

Thuvia. Princess of Ptarth.

Torith. Officer of the guards at submarine pool.

Torkar Bar. Kaolian noble; dwar of the Kaolian Road.

Torquas. A green horde.

Turjun. Carthoris' alias.

Utan. A company of one hundred men (military).

Vas Kor. A Dusarian noble.

Warhoon. A community of green men; enemy of Thark.

Woola. A Barsoomian calot.

Xat. A Martian minute.

Xavarian. A Helium warship.

Xodar. Dator among the First Born.

Yersted. Commander of the submarine.

Zad. Tharkian Warrior.

Zat Arrras. Jed of Zodanga.

Zithad. Dator of the guards of Issus. (See THE GODS OF MARS.)

Zitidars. Mastadonian draught animals.

Zodanga. Martian city of red men at war with Helium.

Zode. A Martian hour.

ABOUT EDGAR RICE BURROUGHS

Edgar Rice Burroughs is one of the world's most popular authors. With no previous experience as an author, he wrote and sold his first novel—*A Princess of Mars*—in 1912. In the ensuing thirty-eight years until his death in 1950, Burroughs wrote 91 books and a host of short stories and articles. Although best known as the creator of the classic *Tarzan of the Apes* and *John Carter of Mars,* his restless imagination knew few bounds. Burroughs' prolific pen ranged from the American West to primitive Africa and on to romantic adventure on the moon, the planets, and even beyond the farthest star.

No one knows how many copies of ERB books have been published throughout the world. It is conservative to say, however, that of the translations into 32 known languages, including Braille, the number must run into the hundreds of millions. When one considers the additional world-wide following of the Tarzan newspaper feature, radio programs, comic magazines, motion pictures and television, Burroughs must have been known and loved by literally a thousand million or more.

"WE ONLY HAVE ONE TEXAS"

People ask if there is really an energy crisis. Look at it this way. World oil consumption is 60 million barrels per day and is growing 5 percent each year. This means the world must find three million barrels of new oil production each day. Three million barrels per day is the amount of oil produced in Texas as its peak was 5 years ago. The problem is that it is not going to be easy to find a Texas-sized new oil supply every year, year after year. In just a few years, it may be impossible to balance demand and supply of oil unless we start conserving oil today. So next time someone asks: "is there really an energy crisis?" Tell them: "yes, we only have one Texas."

ENERGY CONSERVATION – IT'S YOUR CHANCE TO SAVE, AMERICA

Department of Energy, Washington, D.C.

E-